"Mia." Slade's voice was soft.

"Slade, please stop. I'm good."

"You're always good, aren't you? You can conquer the world on your own, right? You don't need us mere mortals to lean on."

"I do. But I don't want to cry over it."

"You're more than this job."

She knew that. She had the list. Daughter. Sister. Granddaughter. "So I've been told. But could someone please tell me who I am?"

He smiled at her, an easy cowboy smile replacing the soft look of sympathy. He'd always had that easy charm.

"Mia, you have to figure out who you are without the job. I can tell you who I think you are. You are the strongest woman I know. You're so strong, you've never seemed to need any of us. You plow through life taking on the world's problems."

"I'm not that strong." She wasn't—she just pretended, and somehow managed to convince herself.

Books by Brenda Minton

Love Inspired

BRENDA MINTON

started creating stories to entertain herself during hour-long rides on the school bus. In high school she wrote romance novels to entertain her friends. The dream grew and so did her aspirations to become an author. She started with notebooks, handwritten manuscripts and characters that refused to go away until their stories were told. Eventually she put away the pen and paper and got down to business with the computer. The journey took a few years, with some encouragement and rejection along the way—as well as a lot of stubbornness on her part. In 2006 her dream to write for Love Inspired Books came true. Brenda lives in the rural Ozarks with her husband, three kids and an abundance of cats and dogs. She enjoys a chaotic life that she wouldn't trade for anything—except, on occasion, a beach house in Texas. You can stop by and visit at her website, www.brendaminton.net.

The Cowboy Lawman
Brenda Minton

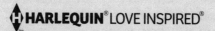

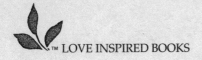 LOVE INSPIRED BOOKS

Recycling programs
for this product may
not exist in your area.

ISBN-13: 978-0-373-87805-5

THE COWBOY LAWMAN

www.LoveInspiredBooks.com

Printed in U.S.A.

And we know that all things work together for good
to them that love God, to them who are the called
according to his purpose.
—*Romans* 8:28

To my kids, because they remind me daily
that without them, I'd…have a clean house.
And be very lonely living in it.

Chapter One

Mia Cooper stood on her porch surveying the quiet landscape of Dawson, Oklahoma. Leaves were turning, the grass had long since dried from lack of rain, and the neighborhood kids had gone back to school weeks ago. She felt alone in the world.

It shouldn't bother her. She knew how to handle loneliness. Even as a Cooper, surrounded by family, she had sometimes felt alone. She also knew how to adjust. She'd been told recently that her strongest skills were her ability to readjust or reinvent herself.

And her biggest detriment.

She just had to decide who she would be now that she was back in Dawson, at her mom's insistence. Okay, she admitted she had been easy to convince. She'd been ready to come home. Her apartment in Tulsa had been too quiet, too private, even for her.

She adjusted the sling that kept her right arm close to her chest, swallowed another gulp of water and jogged down the steps. She could run. She could take to the streets of Dawson, smile and wave to neighbors who might be out. She could pretend that everything would be okay.

But Butch Walker was dead.

That would never change. Butch's wife, Tina, would raise two children alone. Mia would forever remember his face as he went down. She would always live with shooting too late, with not being able to save him.

Her arm might ache. The possibility of not being able to go back to work hurt. But Butch gone—that hurt worse. She could take the pain of running.

She hit the pavement, taking it slow, breathing deep and easy as she lengthened her strides. She swallowed past the tightness in her throat and ignored the pain in her arm and shoulder.

Don't ignore the pain, her doctor had warned her after surgery a month ago. How could she ignore it? It was a constant reminder.

A car came up behind her, and she stepped to the side of the road. Her heart jumped a few paces ahead as she glanced back to make sure it was someone she knew. In Dawson it was rare to see a stranger. Even people you didn't know well weren't considered strangers—they were just people you should get to know better.

Her brother, Jackson, pulled alongside her, the truck window sliding down. She kept running. The truck idled along next to her.

"Jogging, really?" He leaned a little, glanced at the empty country road ahead of them and then looked her way again.

"Yeah, I needed to get out. Alone." She smiled, but it took effort.

"Right. You've never liked too many people in your business. But you have family. Mom has been trying to call you."

She slowed to a fast walk. "I'll call her."

"Today. You can't outrun this."

The big brother in his voice shook her. She remembered a time when she'd been the older sister taking care of her biological siblings, making sure they ate, got dressed each day, survived. Her name then had been Mia Jimenez. And then her mother had died and she'd become the little sister, with people taking care of her. Mia Cooper. Reinvented at age seven.

She and her siblings had been separated.

"Mia, stop running."

"I'll call her." She stopped and closed her eyes, his words sinking in. She'd always been running. Always running from life, from the past, from pain.

The truck stopped next to her. "Mia, you're strong. You're going to survive this."

"I know." She blinked quickly, surprised by the sting of tears. She should have stayed in Tulsa. But as much as her family suffocated her at times, she needed them. Her mom had brought her home on Monday.

"Want a ride home?"

She shook her head and somehow looked at him, smiling as if everything was fine. "No, I can make it."

"Okay, but be safe."

"I'm safe."

He smiled, nodded and shifted to drive away. Mia stood on the side of the road in a world with nothing but fields, trees and the occasional cluster of grazing cattle. A light wind blew, the way wind blew in Oklahoma, and the air smelled of drying grass and blacktop.

Jackson's truck turned a short distance ahead, but his words had opened the wound. Tears blurred her vision and her throat burned. She kept jogging. She kept pushing.

She brushed at the tears that continued to flow. It ached. It ached every minute of every day. Even in her dreams it hurt. She stopped running and looked up at the clear blue sky, at birds flying overhead.

"It hurts!" she yelled as loudly as she could. And then more quietly: "Make it stop. Make it all go away."

There was no answer. Of course there wasn't. God had stopped listening. For some reason He had ignored her when she pleaded for help, holding her hand on Butch's chest, trying to stop the flow of blood, crying as she told him to hold on.

She closed her eyes and slowly sank to her knees in the grass on the shoulder of the road, not caring who came by, what people said about her. It didn't matter. Why should it matter when she hadn't been able to save her partner, her friend's life?

A car pulled up behind her. She didn't turn. She didn't want to know who had found her like this.

A door shut. Footsteps crunched on the gravel shoulder of the road. She wiped a hand across her face and looked up at the person now standing in front of her, blocking the sun, leaving his face in shadows. He smiled a little but his dark gray eyes mirrored her sorrow. He held out a hand.

"It gets easier." His voice was gruff but soft.

"Does it?" She didn't think it would. Today it felt as if it would always hurt like this.

She took his hand.

"Yeah, it does. Is this your first cry?"

She nodded and the tears started again. His hand clasped her left hand. She stood and he pulled her close in an awkward embrace. His hand patted her back and then he stepped away, cleared his throat and looked past her.

"Let me give you a ride home."

She noticed then that he was in his uniform. He'd

been a county deputy for ten years. He'd been the second officer on the scene the night his wife died in a car accident.

"Thanks." She walked back to his car. He opened the passenger-side door for her. Before getting in, she stared up at him, at a face she knew so well. She knew his gray eyes, the way his mouth was strong but turned often in an easy smile. She also knew his pain. "It feels like it might hurt forever."

"I know."

They made the trip back to Mia's in silence. Slade McKennon glanced Mia's way from time to time, but he didn't push her to talk. Their situations were different, but he knew how hard it was to talk when the grief hit, when your throat felt so tight it hurt to take a breath. He knew how hard it was to make sense of it all.

He knew how angry you could get and how every time you opened your mouth, you wanted to yell at God or cry until you couldn't cry any more.

He pulled into her driveway and they sat there a long time, just sitting, staring at her garage in front of them. Finally, she turned to face him, her eyes still watery, rimmed with red from crying. Her dark brown hair framed her face, her normally dark skin looked a shade or two paler.

Tall and slim, athletic, she'd always been an overachiever, the girl who thought she could do it all. And did. She'd been a star basketball player. She'd ridden barrels all the way to nationals, three times. She'd won the whole thing once.

Now she looked as broken as a person could get, but she still had *fighter* written all over her.

"Remember when Vicki used to tell you to just go

ahead and cry?" He smiled as he remembered his wife, her best friend. That was what time did for a person—it made the memories easier, made smiling easier.

"Yeah, she used to do that. When I broke my ankle, sprained my wrist, had a concussion. Cry, she'd say." She rubbed her hand over her face. "But it didn't make sense to cry over it. Pain is an emotion."

Instead of crying, Mia would just get mad. A defense mechanism he guessed from her tough childhood, pre-Coopers. She reached for the door of his patrol car. He knew he wouldn't get much further with her, but he had to try.

"Mia, she would tell you to have faith."

"Don't." She opened the door and looked back at him, one foot on the paved driveway. "Don't give me the easy answers, the platitudes. It doesn't help. I can pray. I can have faith. I can believe in God to do all things. But there is one thing that won't happen."

"I know."

She closed her eyes and the tense lines of her face eased. She reached across the car for his hand and held it tight. "I know you do."

"But I promise you, those words are more than platitudes. It doesn't feel like it right now, but it *is* going to get easier."

"Come in for a cup of coffee?"

Okay, she wanted to change the subject. He radioed in that he'd be out of his car but available on his cell phone. Dispatch responded and he pulled the keys out of the ignition. Yeah, he did that every single time.

Mia saw the keys go in his pocket and she laughed. With watery eyes and red streaks where tears had made trails down her cheeks, she laughed. He smiled and shrugged, he'd take the humiliation if it made her feel better.

"A guy only makes that mistake once." He stepped out of his car.

"You know that Gage and Dylan did that to you."

"Yeah, I know."

Her brothers had hidden his patrol car. He'd been a deputy for two months and those two brothers of hers had spotted his car at the Convenience Counts convenience store, keys in the ignition. He'd been inside grabbing a corn dog and when he walked out, his car was gone. After fifteen minutes of searching on foot, he'd had to radio it in to dispatch. A BOLO, "be on the lookout," for a police car.

Reese Cooper had come along a short time later and told Slade his car was parked at the rodeo grounds. Slade and Reese found the car just as three patrol cars zoomed in.

For several years the other deputies had called him BOLO. They still liked to bring it up from time to time.

Mia met him on the sidewalk, her smile still in evidence.

"Nighttime is the worst," she admitted as she walked up the steps to her front porch.

"I know." He had to tell her why he'd come looking for her. And he wasn't looking forward to it.

"I don't drink coffee," she said as she unlocked the door to her house.

He followed her through the living room to the kitchen. He hadn't been inside her house before today. He didn't know why. He guessed because Vicki and Mia had been best friends. But he and Mia had been friends, too. They'd grown up together. They'd trailered to rodeos together, a bunch of kids sleeping in the backs of trucks and trailers during those two-day events.

After Vicki's death, he'd been wrapped up in making his life work, in being a dad to his infant son, and Mia had taken a job with a DEA drug task force that required undercover work.

He had to tell her why he was here.

In the kitchen she bent to pull a coffeemaker out of the cabinet. He reached to help her. She smiled a little and backed up, letting him put it on the counter.

"What are they saying about your arm?"

She ran the coffeemaker under warm water and then filled it with cold water. He plugged in the machine and stepped back as she did a decent job, left-handed, of pouring water into the reservoir and then fitting a filter into the holder.

"Well, it's held together with a plate and screws. They did what they could for the damaged nerves." She looked down at her splinted wrist and shrugged. "I can start physical therapy pretty soon."

"What about your job?" He measured coffee into the filter and hit the power button. "Will you stay with the DEA?"

She walked away, to the window that overlooked her small yard and the two acres of field. He'd always wondered why she chose this place. She had her own land. Each of the Cooper kids had their own hundred acres.

"I don't know about my job, Slade. The doctors say my right hand will suffer weakness because of the nerve damage." She sighed and didn't turn to face him. "I don't know who I am without that job."

"You're still Mia Cooper."

He moved a few steps and almost, almost put his hand on her shoulder, but he couldn't. She was a friend.

She'd been Vicki's friend. She turned, smiling a sad smile.

"Slade, that's the problem. Who *is* Mia Cooper? For the last few years I've been everyone but the person I thought I was. I've had to pretend to be someone I never wanted to be. I've had to forget myself."

He watched the emotions play across her face, and when she seemed to be looking for herself, she was still Mia. She was still the little sister of Reese, Travis, Jackson, the list went on and on. They were all friends of his. She'd been the kid sister who didn't want to stay at home with the girls. She'd wanted to do the overnight trail rides with the guys. She'd beaten them at basketball, caught bigger fish, ridden harder, played longer.

"You're still Mia. You're stronger than anyone I know. You'll find yourself."

"Stronger than you?" She smiled then, a real smile, a flash of white in a suntanned face. "I don't think so. How's Caleb?"

"He's five now and going to preschool a few days a week. He's a chip off the old block."

"I'll bet he is. I haven't seen him in so long."

"Stop by sometime." He let the words slip out, easy because she was a friend.

"Yeah, I will."

"You've said that before. It would be good for him to know you."

"I want to know him, too."

"I have to go pretty soon." He continued to watch her, slim shoulders straight. She nodded but didn't turn around.

"I'm good." She answered the question he hadn't yet asked.

"No, you aren't. But I'll let you pretend you are."

Now he had to tell her the real reason he'd come looking for her. "Mia, Nolan Jacobs was released from jail last night."

She stood there, not saying a word.

"Mia?"

"I heard you." She faced him, anger flashing in her dark eyes. "What does that mean? He bonded out?"

"I guess so. And the charges have been reduced."

"No. Butch and I covered all our bases. We spent six months living that filthy life, away from our families, pretending to be people we weren't. But he had a way out the whole time. That's how he made us, through an inside source."

"They aren't going to drop this. They won't let you guys down that way."

She leaned against the counter, nearly as tall as he was. She held her right arm and turned to stare out the window for a long minute. Finally, she looked at him.

"What about Butch's wife? Does she know?"

"They're going to tell her." He considered letting it go, but he couldn't. "Mia, it would be best if you went and stayed with your folks for a while. At least until they find a way to bring this guy down."

"That could take a year. It could take two years. I'm not going to live in fear of him, Slade. I'm staying right here in my house. I'm not going to let him win."

She turned and poured coffee into a thermal mug. She handed it to him.

"Thanks." Coffee. It made it seem as if nothing had happened, they weren't talking life and death. They were friends catching up on the news.

"You're welcome."

"And you know I'm going to be out here on patrol.

Wherever that money is that went missing, someone is going to be looking for it."

"You're going to be watching my house? Please don't. I'll feel compelled to feed you and you know I can only cook enchiladas and boxed hamburger meals." She looked down at her arm. "And I can't even cook those right now."

"Maybe I can cook for you." The words slipped out and hung between them.

"Slade…"

He raised a hand to stop her objections. "Friends, Mia, that's what we've always been."

She gave him a curt nod. "Be safe out there, Slade."

"I'm always safe."

She walked with him to the front door. "Yes, I know you are. But I thought we were safe, too. I thought Butch and I would have each other's backs. I thought we'd always be able to save each other."

"You couldn't have known that you'd been made."

"I know." She stood in the front door as he got ready to leave. "Slade, what if I should have known? I keep going over it again and again in my mind, wondering if I saw something that should have given it away."

"Don't. I know that it's easy to second-guess, but it won't change anything."

Slade had done it, too. He'd thought about it over and over, if he should have known what would happen that night to Vicki. He couldn't have known. He'd never seen it coming. But for a couple of years he'd beaten himself up, thinking he should have told her not to drive that night. He should have known there were storms coming.

He should have done something.

For a long minute he stood on Mia's front porch, thinking back. Yes, he knew how Mia felt. He knew the questions she'd been asking herself since the shooting. It took him by surprise when Mia leaned over and kissed his cheek.

"It was an accident."

He touched her arm and smiled down at her. "I know. And I'm asking you to be careful."

"I will."

"Will you be in church Sunday?"

She sighed and shook her head. "So I can yell at God in public? No, I think yelling at Him on the side of the road is enough for one week."

He nodded, because he got it. "If you need anything, call me."

"I'm sure you won't be far away."

"No, I won't."

He walked down the sidewalk to his car, pulling the keys out of his pocket as he went. He glanced back one last time before getting behind the wheel. Mia still stood in the doorway. She wouldn't cry again. He knew Mia. She would walk it off. Or jog it off. And unless people who cared pushed, she wouldn't talk about how much it hurt.

Her family would do that for her. They would push her to talk. And he'd patrol and make sure she stayed safe.

Chapter Two

By Saturday Mia was going stir-crazy. She needed to get out of the house. She needed information and no one had it. And she had definitely tried to get it. She'd called the DEA field office in Tulsa asking questions. Her supervisor had eventually called her back and told her to put her energy into getting better—he'd be the one finding out how Nolan Jacobs had gotten away with murdering one of their agents. Maybe Jacobs hadn't pulled the trigger, but he'd been there. The order to kill had come from him.

She sat at the kitchen table, her laptop in front of her, her cell phone on vibrate. Who had sold them out? She started with a list of people who had been in on their assignment, one that had kept her on the outskirts of Oklahoma City for months when she would have preferred to be anywhere else.

They had lived in a roach-infested apartment, she and Butch. One bedroom, but he'd slept on the couch while they pretended to be husband and wife, small-time dealers wanting in on the big-time. When she left that apartment she'd left behind the clothes, the shoes, the makeup that Maria Vargas, her other identity, had worn.

Maria would have made Mia's mom, Angie Cooper, blush. Maria had made Mia blush a few times. She shook her head, remembering the role she'd played. While in character, she'd looked for family who had lived in Oklahoma City. She'd searched bars and parties for a man who might have been her father. A man with no name but perhaps a tattoo with her mother's name, or even hers.

She'd looked for Breezy and hoped, of all the people she searched for, she wouldn't see her little sister in the crowd, thin from using, near death. She'd never spotted her sibling.

Without really thinking, she went online and put in the last known name of her little sister. Breezy Hernandez. They'd all had different fathers; Mia Jimenez, Juan Lopez and Breezy Hernandez. Juan was in jail for armed robbery and distribution of a controlled substance.

Breezy was the mystery. They'd given her to her paternal grandmother. Angie had learned that much all those years ago. But where they'd gone to—that was the big question. Breezy had disappeared.

The clock in the living room chimed the noon hour. Mia looked at the web page she'd brought up. More dead ends. She closed down her computer and walked to the fridge, to stare again at contents that did nothing for her. She hadn't been hungry in forever.

Because of the burning question: Who had ratted them out? Who had given away information on other law enforcement officers? Who had taken the money and how had they framed Butch?

She closed the fridge and walked through the house.

At the front door, she slipped her feet into flip-flops and shoved money into her pocket. If she didn't have anything good for lunch, Vera at the Mad Cow Café would.

A patrol car eased past her house as she walked out the door. They had all the tact and finesse of boys cruising around on Friday night. Everyone knew what they were up to. And anyone watching Mia would know that the deputies cruised past her house every hour or so. But they cared. They were trying to protect her. In Tulsa they were doing the same for Butch's wife, Tina.

If Nolan came after her, though, he'd know their routine. He'd know their cars. He'd catch her when everyone least expected it.

September air, cool and filled with the scent of drying grass and flowers, greeted her as she walked down the steps of her front porch. The fresh air pulled her back to the present and out of the dark thoughts that had plagued her all morning.

She waved at Mrs. Lucas across the street, one of the few neighbors on this end of Dawson Avenue. *Avenue* was a little overstated. The road led from the feed store to nowhere. There were a total of five houses, most with land. Mr. Gordon raised a few calves. Taylor Green raised sheep. Mrs. Lucas seemed to raise cats, and lots of them.

The cats could usually be found sunning themselves on her porch, and sometimes they moved across the street to Mia's. Mia had never been fond of cats. But she did like Mrs. Lucas, so she didn't complain. As long as the cats didn't bother the birds Mia fed.

It was a short, five-minute walk to the Mad Cow. Mia took it easy, having learned her lesson from her jogging adventure a few days ago. Her arm had ached all night after that little escapade. She'd called her doctor and he'd lectured her about the damage she could have done. Lesson learned.

The parking lot of the Mad Cow was packed with farm trucks, cars and even a couple of tractors.

Mia walked up the sidewalk of the black-and-white-spotted building and someone opened the front door. She smiled at one of the local farmers and he pushed the door wide for her to enter.

"Mia Cooper, been a long time since you was in town. How's that arm doing?" The farmer, Ben, toothpick in the corner of his mouth, smiled and let the door close with both of them inside.

"I'm good." Mia glanced around the crowded diner. She regretted the impulsive decision to come here at noon. People were looking her way. A few whispered.

"Guess you'll be around, getting better after that fall?"

She smiled and didn't correct him on the assumption that she'd fallen. For years people thought she worked at an office in Tulsa and sometimes traveled.

"I'll be around for a while."

Ben pulled the toothpick from his mouth. "You ever think about doing a barrel-racing clinic? I've got a girl who would love to ride. Jackson even has a horse she's interested in. Trouble is, I ain't never been much of a hand with horses."

Barrel-racing clinic?

"Well, I haven't ever thought about it, Ben."

"Well, if you do, you let me know. I can't think of anyone better than a national champion to teach the girls around here."

"Thanks, I'll keep you posted."

The toothpick went back in Ben's mouth, as the conversation seemed to be over. Mia glanced around the crowded restaurant with the black-and-white-tile floors, old Formica-topped tables and booths with seats covered in black vinyl that always got hot and stuck to the back of a person's legs. She loved this place. She remembered the first time she came here with the Coopers. It had been on a Sunday after church.

On that Sunday so long ago, for the first time in her life she hadn't been hungry. That was a memory. She hadn't been the one in charge of making sure everyone ate. She'd sat at the table between Jackson and Reese. Heather had been across from her, smiling, trying to get her to smile. She'd eaten fried chicken. Vera had given her ice cream.

She remembered being afraid that it would all end, that the state would come looking for her and drag her back to her old house. She remembered worrying that wherever Juan and Breezy were, they might not be getting fed, because she wasn't there to care for them.

"Sis, over here." She glanced to the back corner and spotted Jackson and Travis. And Slade McKennon.

Just like old times. But not.

She walked to their booth and Jackson pointed at the seat next to Slade. He scooted and she sat down next to him. His arm brushed hers as he lifted his glass of tea. She reached past him for a menu.

He smelled good. Soap and something like a scent of the Orient tangled up in the mountains of Colorado. She didn't linger but opened the menu and studied a list she'd seen too many times in her life.

"Ben ask you to teach his girl?" Jackson asked, pushing his glass of tea for the waitress to refill.

Travis moved his glass in the same direction. The waitress, a pretty girl with a big smile and blond hair streaked with pink, smiled at Slade. He didn't seem to notice.

"Yes. A barrel-racing clinic? I don't know where he got an idea like that." Mia happened to look up from her menu and her gaze connected with her brother Travis's. And he happened to look quickly at Jackson before taking a bite of biscuits and gravy.

Mia shook her head and refocused from the biscuits covered in sausage gravy to Jackson and his obviously guilty look.

"*You* did this?" She put her menu down and glared at Jackson.

He shrugged. "You might as well."

"Really? Why is it that I *might as well?* I do have a job."

"You're not going to be working for a while. There's a need. You're just about the best."

She arched her brows at him and smiled. "Just about?"

"You *are* the best," he corrected. "Slade, what do you think?"

"I think I don't have a dog in this fight and it's a lot safer that way."

Mia glanced his way, avoiding looking too deep into his gray eyes. She ignored yesterday's five o'clock shadow on the smooth plane of his cheeks. He looked tired.

"Late night?" She looked back to the menu after asking the question.

"Yeah. And an early morning. My mom hasn't been feeling too hot and she won't go to the doctor."

Mia smiled. "That McKennon family stubbornness."

"I guess."

Travis let his fork drop noisily on his plate. "I should get back to the house."

"How's Elizabeth."

"Pregnant?"

"I know that." Mia smiled up at the waitress. "Pueblo salad with ranch. Water to drink."

"Okay." The waitress smiled at Slade again. "You all done with that?"

He passed her his empty plate. Travis held his up and the waitress ignored him and walked off. Mia snorted a laugh and looked at Slade.

"So, is the waitress a friend of yours?" She regretted the question as soon it left her mouth. Talk about testy. She would blame it on lack of sleep.

"No, she isn't." Slade shook his head. "Seriously, Mia, she's barely twenty."

"Right. It's none of my business."

Jackson made a big deal of looking at his watch. "I should go."

Travis slid out after him. "Me, too. I ordered Elizabeth a salad to go and chocolate pie. She's been eating chocolate pie like crazy."

"Tell her to call if she needs anything." Mia reached her hand up and her brother enclosed it in his for a moment. "I can't wait to hold that baby girl."

"I'll pass on the message and if you want to come out and visit, I'll pick you up."

"Thanks, Trav." She smiled past him to Jackson. "And you, I will deal with you later."

Jackson shrugged it off. "You'll thank me later."

After they were gone, she moved to the other side of the booth. Sitting next to Slade while her brothers were there was not a conversation starter. If she stayed next to Slade, the whole town would be talking and speculating.

The swinging doors that led to the kitchen opened. Vera walked out, her dark hair pulled back in a tight bun that looked severe but the smile on Vera's face softened things up.

"Mia Cooper. Honey, I have been praying for you and thinking about you. How'd you like that peanut butter pie I made for you?"

"It was amazing, as always. Mom stayed and had a piece with me."

Vera sat down next to Slade. "Girl, it is so good to see you back. Did you walk down here?"

"It isn't far, Vera."

"Well, no, it isn't. But when you get ready to leave, you holler and I'll bet someone will drive you home. Slade can give you a lift if he's still here."

"I need the exercise." Mia avoided looking at Slade. The waitress had reappeared with a salad topped with grilled chicken, peppers, onions and mushrooms. "That looks great."

"Well, of course it is." Vera cleared her throat. "Do you need any help?"

Mia looked down at the salad, at the fork, at Vera. "No, I'm good."

"Well, I'll let you two catch up and remember to let me know if you need a ride." Vera scooted out of the booth. "Real good to have you home, honey."

Mia smiled and Vera left.

"I don't mind giving you a ride home." Slade leaned back and watched her. He wore a button-up shirt, short-sleeved and dark red. Obviously he wasn't on duty. It deepened his tan. It made his gray eyes look silver.

"I know you don't. I really do enjoy the walk. I think a half a dozen cats followed me to town."

He smiled, teeth flashing white in his suntanned

face. "I heard they discussed the cat issue at a city council meeting."

"She loves those cats, and if the neighbors aren't complaining, why should anyone else?"

Slade shrugged. "There are a lot of them."

"I guess." She took an awkward bite of salad. "This lefty business isn't easy."

No way would she tell him she'd spent the morning loading and unloading her weapon with her left hand. She'd considered taking it out to the ranch for target practice. Just in case.

"Do you need me to cut it up in smaller pieces?"

Her cheeks heated a little and she shook her head. "I'm good."

Slade knew when to be quiet. People either needed the silence or they would fill it up because they needed to talk. Mia ate and ignored him. She knew how to use silence, too. As she ate, he glanced at his watch. He had to pick Caleb up at a friend's house in an hour.

"Go." Mia put her fork down.

"What?"

"You've looked at your watch three times. You're not my keeper. They told you to drive by my house when you're on patrol. They didn't charge you with babysitting."

"I'm not babysitting." He leaned forward a little, lowering his voice. "I'm sitting with a friend while she finishes eating."

"You're starting rumors by sitting here." Mia pushed the plate to the side. "Five years, Slade. You haven't dated in five years. They're all thinking it's about time you did."

"I date. And I don't care if they talk. It's Dawson, that's what we do."

"Right." She reached and tugged at the sling that held her right arm, grimacing. "I hate this thing."

"I know." He reached for the cowboy hat sitting on the back of the booth. It was time to go. He looked around. The waitress hurried their way, pulling out her order pad.

"You all ready to go?" She smiled at him and Slade ignored the foot that kicked his under the table.

"We're all ready. And I'm buying Mia's lunch, too. She's a great date, don't you think?"

"It isn't…"

He stopped Mia's protest. "It isn't our first date."

The waitress turned pink and handed him the two checks. "There you go, Slade. You all need anything else?"

"No, that's good." He slid out of the booth and waited for Mia to join him. "I'll give you a ride home."

Mia stood. "You're real funny."

"You're the one who said I need to start dating. Now if anyone in town is thinking it's time, they'll be satisfied to think that you're the one I'm dating." He winked and a streak of red crawled up her neck. Embarrassed or mad? He guessed he'd find out.

When they walked out the door of the Mad Cow, she slugged his arm. "That's great. I tell you not to start rumors, so you go ahead and start the biggest one you can think of."

Slade led her to his truck. He opened the passenger-side door and turned to face her. "I date."

"Fine, you date." She had that mad look on her face—one brow shot up as her eyes narrowed. "But you don't date me. That's not the way it works."

"She's been gone five years, Mia." His heart still ached when he said it. Man, five years. Caleb was in kindergarten. Slade had a few gray hairs. He'd bought new furniture, finally.

They stood behind the open door of the truck. Mia's eyes watered and she touched his cheek. A snowstorm at that very moment couldn't have surprised him more. It surprised him for a lot of reasons he didn't really want to think about.

"I still miss her," she whispered, leaning close.

"I do, too."

"She would have wanted you to move on." Mia's hand slid off his cheek. "I'm home now, so I can watch Caleb if you want to go out."

"Thanks." He cleared his throat and tried not to think about her offer. "We'd better go. I have to pick Caleb up in thirty minutes."

"Sure, okay."

She climbed in. He pulled the seat belt around her and buckled it. He knew that she held her breath as the buckle clicked. He was also aware of her breath soft on his neck, and the fresh-washed scent of her clothes.

He stepped back.

"Thank you." She gave him a gentle smile and he closed the truck door.

They drove to her house in silence.

"If you want to go to church tomorrow, I can pick you up." He offered as they pulled into her drive and parked.

She didn't answer right away. He shouldn't have offered. If people saw them showing up to church together, the rumors would definitely fly. He figured she had to be thinking the same thing.

"I'm not sure."

"You're not sure if you want me to pick you up or if you're ready to go?"

"Both." She reached for the door handle. "It isn't easy, being this angry. I'm afraid I'll go to church and the message will be directed at me, telling me to forgive myself, forgive God. Or, worse, forgive Nolan Jacobs."

"That's a whole lot of forgiving."

She sighed and the door opened a few inches. "I'm going to find the leak."

"I figure you probably will. But don't get yourself hurt."

"Little late for that." She stepped out of the truck.

Slade followed her to the front door. She stuck her key in the lock and turned the knob. As she pushed the door open she turned to face him.

"I'm going in with you." He reached past her and pushed the door the rest of the way open.

"Slade, Nolan Jacobs is a free man. Do you really think he's going to show up here and ruin that for himself?"

"He might, if he thinks you have information that could put him back in jail. Or if he thinks you have that money."

She stood in the doorway, blocking his entrance. "I'm good, Slade. You have to go."

"Right." He backed away from the door. "Mia, be careful."

"I will. And you be careful, too." She gave him an easy smile, the way she used to.

He wished they could go back in time, just for a little while, and remember what it was like to be young and think the world couldn't hurt them.

She'd be tough, a fighter who rode hard and played hard.

He'd be the guy in love with Vicki, knowing they would be together forever.

Instead they were facing each other as if those other people were strangers, that other life a dream. And dangerous thoughts were going through his mind. The most dangerous of all—what would it be like to kiss Mia Cooper?

In all the years growing up together, they'd never kissed. Not even when they played Truth or Dare. He figured if he ever tried, she'd knock him down.

He'd been Reese's best friend. She'd been Vicki's best friend.

Now they were both alone. He didn't know what that meant but he couldn't let the thought go. Fifteen minutes later when he stopped at the house where Caleb had spent the night and he saw his son running out to greet him, the thought was still there.

He got out of the truck and met Caleb at the edge of the Martins's drive. Mrs. Martin came out to tell him the boys had had a great time. Slade thanked her and picked up his son to put him in the backseat of his truck.

"Dad, I missed you."

"Missed you, too, Cay."

For some crazy reason, "missing" made him think of Mia again. He hadn't realized until she came home that he had missed her.

Chapter Three

The doorbell chimed early Sunday morning. Not exactly sunrise, but Mia hadn't been up long. She had a cup of tea, her computer and a shady spot on the back patio. No one would bother her on Sunday morning.

She left her tea and headed back inside through the house. Before opening the door, she peeked out. She didn't know whether to be relieved when she saw the familiar car in the drive or run for cover.

A face peered in the window at her and she jumped back. Granny Myrna waved and then laughed.

"Open up, Sugar. I need a cup of coffee," Granny Myrna yelled through the window and Mia nodded.

She clicked the dead bolt, turned the lock and opened the door.

"You've got this place locked up tighter than Fort Knox. My goodness." Her grandmother pulled off white lacy gloves and her Sunday hat. "I ran out of coffee and since you're the only Cooper smart enough to live in town, I thought I'd come over here and bug you for a cup."

"You also know that I don't drink coffee." Mia

hugged her grandmother, slipping an arm around her waist as they walked to the kitchen.

"Well, I do know you have a coffeepot and I'm willing to bet you keep some coffee in the house."

"I do have coffee."

"Well, then, I'll just make a pot real quick and how about some breakfast?"

"Gran, you don't have to cook for me. I had yogurt."

"That isn't enough to keep a bird alive. No wonder you're so thin."

"I'm fine."

They reached the kitchen, and Mia's grandmother had coffee going in a matter of minutes.

"I already feel better just smelling the coffee." Granny Myrna gave her the once-over. "You're not dressed for church."

"No, I'm not."

"And why is that?"

Mia glanced away from her grandmother's piercing look, the look that always saw far more than the average person.

"Gran, I'm not ready to go. I can't fix my hair or put on makeup. I can't…"

"Face your pain?" Granny Myrna got right to the heart of things, the way she always did.

"I'm not sure."

"Of course, you are. You know that you're angry. You know that you're hurt. You called out to God and you think he didn't answer. That's understandable. What isn't understandable to me is how the strongest young woman I know could sit in this house and give up."

"I haven't given up."

"No?"

"No." Mia pushed the coffeepot because it was tilted

on the heating element and about to spill out over the lid. "I'm not hiding. I'm just trying to get my head on straight."

"I know that I can't convince you that God was there that night, Mia, but He was. He didn't leave you or ignore you. It just feels that way right now. You might never know why things happened the way they did. You might always feel a little angry, a little confused. But God can get you through the anger, too."

"I love you, Gran."

"Of course you do. I'm very easy to love. And I'm almost always right. Now don't tell people I confessed to the 'almost' part. I'm just sharing that with you, and I'll deny it if you tell anyone."

"I won't tell a soul."

"Then come to church with me. You can take your anger there. It's safe. And you might find a little peace to go with the anger."

"You're pushy."

"It's one of the perks of being eighty-five. And we have plenty of time. I'll have coffee, you drink that nasty tea of yours and then I'll help you get ready."

Mia leaned to kiss her grandmother's softly wrinkled cheek. "I am so glad you're my grandmother."

"Oh, honey, I'm so very glad you're my granddaughter. And by the way, now that you're home for a little while, maybe you can do something about Slade McKennon."

"Why?"

"He's far too good-looking to be eating alone at the Mad Cow. Don't you think?"

"I'll try to think of someone to fix him up with." She smiled as she wiped up the counter. She knew that wasn't what her grandmother meant, but it was all she could handle right now.

"You would want him to date someone else?"

"Gran, Slade is my friend—nothing more." She thought about his hand on hers, and the memory took her by surprise. She and Slade had always been just friends. They'd shared a childhood, shared memories, shared grief.

The thought of anything more with Slade... She shook her head. Slade belonged to Vicki.

She led her grandmother to the patio and the two of them sat down. The sun had climbed higher and their shade wouldn't last much longer. Mia closed her computer to keep her grandmother from seeing too much. Not that Mia had found anything. Breezy didn't seem to exist.

What if something had happened to her sister? What if...

She picked up her cup and took a drink of the now-tepid tea. The thought that Breezy might be gone, perhaps had been gone for years without Mia knowing, continued to haunt her.

"Mia?"

She opened her eyes and smiled at her grandmother. The confession slipped out. "I'm searching for my sister."

Granny Myrna set her coffee down with a thunk, slopping the brown liquid over the edge of the cup onto the table.

"Well, that wasn't what I expected."

Mia half smiled. "I know. I've tried over the years but now that I have plenty of time, I'm really digging."

"But not finding her?"

"No."

"You will. You're the best detective I know."

"Do you know a lot of detectives, Gran?"

"Well, not many, but you're the best." Her grandmother glanced at the delicate watch that had been her eightieth-birthday present from Tim and Angie Cooper. "We need to get you ready to go."

Mia looked down at her sweats and the T-shirt she'd pulled on that morning. "This doesn't work for you?"

"Let's see if we can't find a skirt to pull on with that shirt and not the sweatpants that I think you wore for gym class a dozen years ago."

"They're comfy."

"They do look comfy, but no." Granny Myrna stood and gathered up their cups. "Let's get this show on the road."

Mia left the house fifteen minutes later looking what her grandmother called "presentable" in a peasant skirt, flip-flops and the dark red T-shirt she'd put on that morning. Her hair was pulled back in a ponytail and Granny Myrna had even done a decent job with lip gloss and mascara.

When they pulled into the church parking lot, Mia felt a sense of coming home mixed with a healthy dose of nerves. She looked up at the steeple and thought about all the angry words she'd screamed the night Butch died in her arms. She thought about bargains she'd made, bargains that God had ignored.

"Time to go in." Her grandmother pulled the keys out of the ignition. "All to Jesus, I surrender."

Mia gathered her purse and Bible. "Even anger?"

"Even anger."

They walked up the steps of the church, her grandmother holding the rail. Mia slowed her steps, realizing with an ache that her granny didn't move as quickly as she used to. In the spring she'd even had a few mini-strokes.

At the top of the steps stood Slade McKennon and his little boy, Caleb. She smiled at the five-year-old boy with the blond hair because it was easier to look at him than at his father. Caleb, Vicki's baby.

She remembered holding him at Vicki's funeral, cuddling him close. When she looked up from Caleb to meet Slade's gray eyes, she knew that he'd gone back in time, too. He managed a smile. Hers was slower to return.

"Good to see you here."

"Thank you." She looked past him into the church. "It's good to be here."

Behind her, Granny Myrna prodded her forward. "Slade and Caleb are going to ring the bell. We need to find a seat."

Find a seat? Mia smiled at that. The Coopers sat on the second pew from the front. It wasn't their pew. If visitors showed up, the Cooper clan moved. But most of the time, you'd find them there, sitting together. A few of the kids missed church from time to time. Heather went to church in Grove. She liked the anonymity of going to a big church. Blake Cooper, second to the oldest of the kids, sometimes had business that kept him out of town.

Gage and Dylan traveled a lot, bull riding or providing livestock for rodeos and bull rides. Bryan, the youngest brother, was in South America on a mission trip.

Mia called it his "guilt trip." He had made a mistake, like so many other kids, and now he felt he had to pay for it.

Caleb reached for her hand as she eased past father and son. "Do you know I'm in school now?"

She smiled down at him. "I heard that. Do you like it?"

Vicki had always wanted half a dozen kids. Caleb should have been one of many. Mia had always groaned at the idea of six kids. She'd grown up as a Cooper, surrounded by siblings.

Caleb nodded. "We're having a class party and the moms are bringing cupcakes."

"That's going to be great." Mia looked up from the little boy to his dad.

"Let Mia go, Caleb. We'll talk to her later."

Caleb released her hand. Mia knelt next to him and wrapped her left arm around him in a quick hug. "I think I know how to make cupcakes."

He smiled at that but Slade cleared his throat. "We've got it covered."

Mia got it. Slade didn't want her that involved in his life. She stood and followed her grandmother down the aisle to the second pew from the front.

Slade watched Mia walk down the aisle toward the front of the church. He didn't know why it hurt him so much to watch her with Caleb. He guessed because it had hurt five years ago when she sat behind him at Vicki's funeral, holding their baby boy. But today was different. Today something else had happened when he saw her hug his son. This was a different kind of ache.

It took him by surprise and he stood there for a full minute trying to make sense of it. A hand reached for his and pulled hard.

He looked down at Caleb and smiled.

"You going to hand me that rope?" Caleb stood steady in his new boots and his best shirt.

"I sure am." Slade unhooked the rope from the hook on the wall and handed it to his son. "Ring the bell, Caleb."

Caleb pulled hard, swinging a little on the rope and then pulled again. The sound of the ringing bell filled the Sunday-morning silence. It was a constant, that bell. It ranked with Sunday lunch, good friends, Vera's fried chicken and weekends at the rodeo.

After Caleb finished ringing the bell, Slade followed his son down the aisle to the empty spaces they'd left behind the Coopers. Slade's mom hadn't shown up yet. He glanced at his watch. She was never late. Caleb slid into the pew and Slade sat next to him. He glanced at his watch and then at his silenced phone.

In front of him Mia reached to smooth her dark hair. He watched as she settled nervously, waiting for the service to start. He remembered the day he returned to church. It took him a month, maybe six weeks after Vicki's accident. Looking back, he shouldn't have waited. He'd avoided the place and people he had needed most.

His mom had tried to tell him that. He hadn't wanted to listen. Now, with Caleb next to him, he realized they had survived. It still hurt, but they were making it. They were good, the two of them.

Lately his mom had been telling him that no one could take Vicki's place, but that didn't mean he couldn't find room in his heart for love. Caleb squirmed next to him, digging in his pocket for something, distracting Slade from uncomfortable thoughts. He looked down at his son, frowning as the kid pulled something from his pocket.

No way. He shook his head at the half-eaten piece of taffy. It had lint stuck to it and probably bacteria that would light up a microscope. Caleb gave the candy a wistful look and handed it over. Now what in the world was he supposed to do with it? Slade sighed and fisted the candy. A tissue got tossed over his shoulder. He smiled back at Ryder Johnson and his wife, Andie. She grinned and blew a kiss at Caleb. Their twin girls were in the church nursery.

Life in Dawson was changing. Slade had come to terms with the reality that he and his friends were now the adults in town and there were new kids sitting on the tailgates of trucks parked at the local convenience store.

His phone buzzed in his pocket. He ignored it the first time. It rang again. A slow, bad feeling slid into his chest. He put a finger to his lips to silence Caleb and pointed for him to stay. He reached up, tapping Miss Myrna Cooper on the shoulder. When she turned he showed her his phone and pointed to Caleb. She nodded.

The congregation started to sing and Slade hurried down the aisle to the doors. His phone was ringing a fourth time as he stepped outside.

"Slade McKennon."

"Slade, it's Janie, on the ambulance. Hon, we've got your mom here. She's having chest pains. We're going to head for Grove Hospital if you want to meet us there."

The tightness that had grabbed hold of him when the phone rang twisted a little tighter. "I'll be right there."

"Now, Slade, your mom says for you not to drive like a maniac. She's fine. I agree with her. Don't rush. She's going to be in the E.R. and getting good care, so you take it easy."

He closed his eyes and took a deep breath. "I'll take

it easy. Tell her I'm going to find someone to watch Caleb and I'll be there in twenty minutes."

Janie laughed a little. "Your mom said it better take you longer than twenty minutes."

He slid the phone back into his pocket and stepped back into the church, where he nearly bumped into Mia Cooper. She wasn't smiling.

"What's up?"

He slid a hand across her back and followed her back outside. "They're taking my mom to the E.R. She's having chest pains. I need to make arrangements for Caleb and go."

"Do you want me to take care of Caleb or go with you?"

"Mia, you don't have to…"

She cut him off with a glare. "I'm either taking care of that little boy or I'm going with you. It's your choice which one I do."

"Can you watch Caleb?" He looked away, just for a minute, needing to ground himself.

"I think I can manage one five-year-old boy, Slade."

"I know you can." He glanced at his watch. "I'll call you later."

"That's good. And Slade, I'll pray for her."

It took him by surprise, the softness in her voice, in her expression. It drew him in and he leaned to kiss her cheek. "Thank you."

She blinked a few times, then let it go. "Call me when you know something."

"I will. Tell Caleb his grandma is good. She even told me not to drive fast. He doesn't need to worry."

"I'll tell him."

She slipped back inside the church, closing the door softly behind her. Slade stood there, staring at the double doors for a few seconds before he turned and hurried down the steps and across the parking lot toward his truck. His better self took control, not letting him think too much about Mia and the decision to leave his son in her care.

As he pulled out of the parking lot, his mind was fully planted on his mom and her health. Anything could happen. In the blink of an eye, the world could change. He'd experienced it. His mom had, too. Ten years ago when they lost his dad to cancer.

The roads were quiet. A typical Sunday morning in Dawson. Most people were in church. There were only a couple of cars at Vera's. He drove out of town, speeding up as he left the city limits behind. He hit his emergency flashers and punched the gas, forgetting the twenty-minute rule his mom had set.

He had kissed Mia on the cheek. He shook his head and called himself a few names because kissing Mia had always been off-limits. He'd always been okay with that rule. What had changed?

Chapter Four

After church, and after making a few excuses to avoid lunch at Cooper Creek Ranch, Mia led Caleb across the parking lot to her grandmother's car. The child held tight to her left hand. His feet dragged.

"You know, it's easier to walk if you lift your feet."

"Is my grandma okay?" He looked up from the blacktop he'd been studying. His blue eyes narrowed on her as he waited for an answer.

"She's going to be just fine. She's at the hospital and they'll give her medicine to help her heart."

"Is it attacking her?"

She hid a smile at the image he probably had in his mind.

"It's hurting."

"I'm going to your house?" He looked down again. She got it. He barely knew her. A few visits over the years wasn't a lot.

She sighed and then squatted in front of him to put herself at eye level. "Caleb, your grandma is okay and your dad is going to pick you up at my house. We'll hang out together and maybe we can convince your dad to bring pizza later."

"Do you have toys?"

She grinned. "I have a few trucks that my nieces and nephews play with at my house."

"Girls play with trucks?" He wrinkled his nose.

"Yeah, they do."

"Okay." He looked up and grinned, but not at her. "Hi, Jackson."

She glanced back and then up, frowning at her brother. "I'm going with Gran."

He raised his hands in surrender. "I know and I wasn't going to try to talk you into going to the house. I wanted to see if I could keep a mare at your place."

"A mare? Because you don't have room for one more?" They both knew that wasn't the case. She held out a hand and Jackson pulled her to her feet.

"I picked her up from a place north of Grove. The owners lost their farm and went to Tulsa. She's been in a corral for a few weeks and needs to be stabled and have some weight put on her."

A broken horse to fix. She knew this game. When she'd first moved to Cooper Creek twenty years ago, she'd been given a sick goat to care for. She had kept that goat for years. That goat, crazy as it seemed, had probably saved her life.

"Jackson, I don't need a project."

His eyes widened. "Who said it was a project?"

"I know you too well. You're the guy who led me out to the barn and told me that the sick goat wouldn't live if someone didn't take care of it."

"It lived, didn't it?"

"Yeah, it did." And so had she.

She remembered her mother lying on the floor, OD'd, and police moving through the house. She'd hidden her siblings under a bed because it had always been her job to protect them. She shivered even with the warmth of the sun pouring down on her.

"Mia?"

"Bring it by tomorrow."

"Thanks." Jackson ruffled Caleb's hair. "Later, buddy. Don't let Mia get you into trouble."

The little boy looked up at Jackson and grinned big, probably thinking trouble sounded like fun.

Her grandmother finally joined them, looking a little spacey, smiling like a woman with a secret. And Mia knew that it had to do with an old farmer named Winston. Her grandmother, at eighty-five, was in love.

Love? Mia shook her head as she opened the back door of the sedan for Caleb to climb in. Love wasn't her thing. She'd tried it once, but the man in question hadn't been able to handle a woman in law enforcement with a gun and better aim than him.

Not that she had a career now. It still didn't mean she wanted romance with flowers and moonlit walks. No, that wasn't her cup of tea. She'd never really dated. In high school she preferred the easy camaraderie of her brothers and their friends to the complicated relationships her friends seemed to seek out.

She slid into the front seat of the car and glanced back at Caleb. His attention was focused on the window, but she saw worry reflected in his eyes. Stoic. She got it. She knew how it worked. If you didn't talk about it, it didn't hurt. Or so she'd always tried to convince herself.

"What do you want for lunch?" she asked and he turned from the window to face her.

"I like peanut butter."

"That sounds good. I like mine grilled with strawberry jam. Have you ever had grilled peanut butter and jelly?"

"That sounds gross."

She smiled. "Yeah, I guess it does. But it tastes good."

He turned back to the window. "I'd like to see that horse."

"Huh?" She looked out the window, but she didn't see a horse.

"The horse Jackson has."

"Oh, okay. I'll have your dad bring you by to see it."

"Okay. And I'd eat that sandwich."

Granny Myrna chuckled but she didn't say anything. Mia shot her a look. "What?"

"Nothing." The older woman shifted into Drive and eased the car forward. "I'll help you make those sandwiches."

"I can do it. You go ahead and have lunch with the family."

"Two of us can skip out on the interrogation."

Mia smiled. "So you're avoiding questions about Winston."

"That I am. And you've been avoiding the inevitable for years."

"What does that mean?"

Mia's grandmother kept driving. "Mia, you have to stop running."

"I have. The doctor told me…"

Granny Myrna gave her a full-blown angry look. "I am not talking about actual running. I'm talking about facing your life, your past and all that stuff you've bottled up inside you that you pretend you've dealt with."

"Oh." Mia didn't know what else to say. She could argue, but arguing with her grandmother never worked. Granny Myrna would remind Mia that at eighty-five she had lived a lot and seen a lot.

"Is that all you have to say?"

Mia glanced back at Caleb. He was sound asleep.

"Gran, I'm good."

"No, you're not. You're good at avoiding, but that isn't good. You watched your mother die. You lost your siblings. You've lost a lot."

"I have people who love me. I have a family." And she'd never been one to dwell on the past. "I've lost, but I've gained, too."

"Yes, you do have people who love you, and I'm one of them. But I think you stay as busy as possible and you hold yourself back for fear of losing again."

"Have you been watching Dr. Phil again?" Mia admitted to herself the joke was getting old. But her grandmother's words ached deep inside and she didn't want to explore her feelings today, tomorrow or anytime soon.

They had reached Mia's house and Granny Myrna pulled up to the garage and parked. "You need to think about what I've said."

"I will."

"And I am going to come in and fix you both sandwiches."

"Thanks, Gran."

Mia managed to wake Caleb up. He rubbed his eye a few times and blinked. "Is the horse here?"

She reached for his hand. "No. Let's go in and have lunch. The horse won't be here until tomorrow."

"Oh. I think I had a dream."

"Did you?"

He nodded as Mia opened the door wider for him to get out. "Yeah, we were riding that horse faster than Uncle Gray's motorcycle."

"That would be something, huh? Someday maybe we'll ride her."

"Soon?" He rubbed his face again and yawned.

"Yeah, soon."

They walked up the steps of the porch, Granny Myrna in the lead. When they reached the door she turned and looked back at Mia and Caleb.

"Didn't you lock this door?"

Mia's neck hairs tingled and the sensation slid down her spine. She stopped Caleb and at the same time reached for her grandmother, pulling her back lightly.

"Yes, I did." She always locked her doors. Out of habit she reached for her sidearm. But she didn't have one. She stepped toward the door, listening. She leaned against the door frame, motioning her grandmother back. Her weapon was in the house. Locked up, but if a person didn't mind breaking down a front door, he wouldn't have a problem breaking into a gun cabinet.

"Mia, I'm calling 911." Her grandmother's voice shook as she whispered from a few feet away.

Mia eased through the door. "Stay here and don't touch anything."

She could hear her grandmother already talking to the 911 operator. Mia stepped farther into her living room.

The cushions were off the sofa and the end tables had been ransacked. She stood in one spot, listening. Nothing. She eased through the house, room by room. Whoever had been here was gone now.

But someone had definitely been in her house, in her sanctuary, the place she'd kept separate from her job, that life. This had been her place of light, away from the dark world that always felt too much like her childhood.

A world she kept going back to, even though she'd escaped from it.

A car pulled up. A radio squawked. Mia walked out

the front door and met a county deputy coming up the sidewalk.

"The house is clear." She motioned him inside.

"You went in?" He stepped to the door, pushing it open with his gloved hand. "No sign of forced entry."

Another car cruised down the road and pulled in. She smiled at Caleb, standing next to her, thinking to reassure him. He appeared to be having the time of his life. At five, everything was an adventure. She did have a moment's hesitation when she thought about explaining this to Slade.

The second car was unmarked. The trooper nodded to Mia's grandmother and to Caleb.

"I'd like for you all to take a seat in my car until we've looked the house over."

"Jim, the house is clear." Mia protested and the trooper shook his head.

"Mia, I'm asking you to let us do our job." He pointed to his car. She sighed and headed that way with her grandmother and Caleb. "I'm going, but not because I want to."

He laughed as he walked through her front door. "Mia, I wouldn't expect anything else from you."

"What's going on?" Caleb slid into the backseat of the sedan.

"Just being careful, Caleb." Mia stood outside, peering in at her grandmother and Slade's son. She had put them in danger. She should have gone to the ranch after church, then none of this would have happened. She could have come home alone, noticed the unlocked door and handled things herself.

The boy leaned forward, watching her house through the window. "But why?"

Oh, yes, the *questions*. She remembered that with

Bryan, her youngest brother and with a few foster children the Coopers had taken in over the years. She knew he wouldn't stop until he had answers.

"Because my front door was open and because it's always good to be careful."

"Oh."

She stepped away from the car door. "I'm going to make a phone call."

Her grandmother peered a little too closely. Mia never liked that look. It felt too much like her grandmother knew what she was up to. And Myrna Cooper usually did.

Mia dialed her phone as she walked away from the car. She waited and finally a soft voice said, "Hello."

"Tina, it's Mia. I wanted to check on you." She watched as another vehicle came up the road. Slade's truck. She hadn't wanted this. He should be in Grove at the hospital.

"Mia, I…"

"Tina, what?" Mia's back tingled and she waited, holding her breath. "Are you and the kids okay?"

"Of course. Yes, we're fine."

Mia stood there for a long moment. She watched Slade get out of his truck and walk to the car where Caleb still waited, jumping out when he saw his dad. She watched Myrna explain what had happened. Slade looked her way, his eyes narrowing, his mouth tightening in a firm line. He took off his hat and ran a hand through his short, dark hair.

The tightness in her chest eased and she breathed a little easier. Because Slade was there? She shook it off and returned to Tina and the conversation that had lagged.

"Tina, maybe you should come visit me."

"No, I don't think so, Mia. I'm fine. Really I am."

"I'll stop by and see you in a few days." Mia waited and knew that Tina would protest.

"You really don't have to do that."

"I know I don't, but I have a doctor's appointment and I'll be in Tulsa. I think it would be great if we could have lunch, maybe take the kids out."

"That would be good. We'll talk then."

Slade had put his son and her grandmother back in the patrol car. He stood in front of her, hands behind his back, handsome cowboy face a mask of concern. Her eyes connected with his. She wanted to look away because if anyone could read her, it was Slade. She looked away as she finished the conversation.

"We'll talk, Tina. And call if you need anything. Anything at all." She hung up, but made a mental note to call her boss in Tulsa.

"What's going on?" Slade asked the minute she slipped the phone into her pocket.

"How's your mom? You should be with her." Mia watched as the officers went back into her house.

"My mom had a heart attack. Mild, but she's going to need to rest. My sister is with her now." His gaze shifted, taking in his son. Mia knew this would be hard. Slade's mom had been the person filling in since Vicki's death.

"I can watch him for you." The words were out, no taking them back.

Slade turned, looking at her. "What?"

"Caleb." Mia hesitated as she looked at the child sitting next to her grandmother. "If your mom needs to rest, she isn't going to be able to do that with a five-year-old child in the house. I can watch him for you."

"I don't know." He glanced at her arm but she thought that was just an excuse.

"I can handle a kid in my house." She looked up into his silver-gray eyes.

Friendship. Easy. Uncomplicated. No problem.

The officers approached, both looking more relaxed now that they'd been through her house and found it safe. She could have told them it was safe. She was injured—that didn't mean she'd forgotten how to do her job.

"We bagged some evidence." The trooper shrugged. "But it isn't much. We got a partial print."

"I told you…"

Slade touched her arm, stopping her.

"Mia, they're doing their job."

"Any idea who or why?" the deputy asked.

Mia shook her head, but she did have ideas. And she had a really sick feeling in the pit of her stomach that it had something to do with Tina.

But who did she trust with that information? Her eyes sought Slade's. He was watching her, suspicious, curious, concerned. Maybe all three.

She knew she could trust Slade.

Slade watched the patrol cars leave and then he walked with Mia, Myrna Cooper and Caleb to the house. Myrna fanned herself with a church bulletin she pulled out of her purse.

"Well, that's more excitement than an old gal needs in one day. Slade, how's your mama doing?"

"She'll be released tomorrow, but they want her to rest. Not that she's going to be okay with resting."

"Well, I'll take a casserole over there tomorrow afternoon. You tell her not to worry about a thing."

Caleb's face scrunched and he looked at his dad. "Is grandma okay?"

"She's fine, Caleb. Her heart is a little sick but the doctors will help it get better."

He hoped that was the truth. It had to be. He had prayed long and hard on the way to the hospital. The prayers had taken him back to the night Vicki died. He'd prayed that he would get to the accident and it would be a mistake, that it wouldn't be her. The old wound opened, and he had to reach down for his son's hand to jolt himself back to the present.

Caleb smiled up at him, squeezing his hand back. For years, it had been the two of them against the world. And Slade's mom had helped him hold it all together.

Caleb pulled on his hand, forcing him to follow Mia into the house. She walked through the living room that had been turned upside down to the kitchen door and then stood, lost in her own thoughts. He watched her, and she caught his look and held it before smiling at his son.

"We should eat lunch. Caleb and I were going to have grilled PB&J." She made it sound normal, like nothing had happened. Mia had experience dealing with what life threw at her.

He looked at his son, surprised by the choice. "Did you let her talk you into that?"

Caleb grinned big. "Granny Myrna says it's better than it sounds."

"If she says so, it probably is." He caught a look from Myrna and he wasn't quite sure what to make of it. He definitely didn't think it had anything to do with grilled peanut butter and jelly. That was just a guess on his part.

"It's always good to trust my judgment, Slade Mc-

Kennon. I've lived a long time and I have a few things figured out."

"Like grilled PB&J?"

"Exactly." Myrna looked at her watch. "Well, my goodness, I didn't realize it had gotten so late. I'm going to have to run. Slade, do you think you could help Mia out?"

Before he could answer, Mia rushed into the conversation. "Gran, I can take care of things. You go and I'll be fine."

"Slade is here. He won't mind helping you." Granny Myrna winked at Slade. "Isn't that right?"

She headed for the door and Slade couldn't think as fast as she seemed to be able to walk. He reached the door just in time to open it so that she could make a grand exit, smiling back at him and waving her fingers.

"You kids be good, and I'll be back tomorrow to check on you, Mia."

With that she was gone.

"She's good." Mia laughed as she said it.

He turned and Mia stood a few steps behind him with that look on her face that said she could handle anything. But if he looked closer, into dark eyes that shadowed and closed a person out, maybe she wasn't handling things after all.

"You okay?"

"Why would you ask that?"

"Do you want me to make a list of reasons why you wouldn't be okay? Should I start with your partner dying in your arms? Follow that with an injury that might mean the end of your career, then we'll talk about someone breaking into your house. Have I missed anything?"

She shook her head, "No, you cut right to the heart of it. Thanks."

"Mia, we're friends. I'm here. And I know that you're going to try to bury all this and pretend nothing happened. It's better to talk it out."

"I know." Her voice grew soft and she turned away. "We should fix lunch. I'll bet Caleb is starving. Where is Caleb?"

"He's in the kitchen."

She nodded but kept her back to him. "Let's get that boy something to eat."

He reached for her left arm. "Mia, stop."

She still didn't turn. Back ramrod-straight and head high, she stood frozen beneath his touch. "Slade, I'm barely hanging on right now. I'm not sure who was in my house or what they were looking for. Butch is dead and Tina is hiding something."

Her voice broke and he moved to face her. Her eyes closed and she shook her head when he rested his hand on her shoulder. He stepped back, giving her space to find strength. She took a deep breath and opened her eyes.

"Slade, I have to figure this out."

"I'll help."

"You have your plate pretty full with Caleb, your mom and your job."

He laughed a little at that. "And you volunteered to watch Caleb. I won't hold you to that."

"I want to watch him."

"I don't know." He brushed a hand across his face, suddenly bone-tired and wishing he could have a do-over on this day.

"How do we move on, Slade? How do we stop holding on to the past? You're holding on to Caleb because he's all you have left of Vicki. I've been afraid to look at him, get attached to him, because he's all I have left of my best friend. I should have been in his life, hugging him and being the person Vicki would have wanted me to be."

"We did what we had to do to survive."

"Right." Mia looked down at her right arm, held tight to her body with the sling. "Now what?"

"Last time I checked, you haven't stopped surviving. Maybe you've lost some faith, but you're going to get that back."

"Will I?"

"Yeah, you will. Take it from someone who had to dig hard to find God when I needed Him most. And now I can look back and realize I should have let Him back in a lot sooner. I should have spent less time angry."

"Anger's easier than the pain."

Yeah, the pain. He remembered when it had been fresh, cutting like a hot knife into his heart. He'd thought it would last forever. It still hurt, but not like that. Not all the time.

He knew Mia would get there, too.

She let out a long sigh. "Slade, I could really use a hug."

Mia, a hug? She smiled at him, because she had to know what he was thinking.

"Even I need a hug once in a while, McKennon."

He raised his arms, awkward, really awkward. Mia stepped into his embrace. He stood there for a few long seconds unsure about what to do next. And then his arms circled her. She breathed in and rested her head on his shoulder and her left arm went around his waist.

Awkwardness dissolved and he rested his hand on her back.

"I hate this," she murmured against his collar. "I hate being weak. I hate not having answers. I hate not being able to fix it."

"I know." He kissed the top of her head and she backed up, wiping at her eyes.

"I'm not a blubbering baby."

"I know that, too. And if I remember correctly, you were with me when I lost it a few times."

"You were there for me, too."

"I guess I was."

Friends, sitting on the tailgate of a truck at the back of a field, holding hands and crying over the loss of a wife, the loss of a best friend.

"I wasn't married to Butch, Slade. What you went through… I know you still miss her."

"I miss her. I miss who we would have been together. I miss the moments she would have had with Caleb." Slade took hold of Mia's hand and led her into the kitchen. Caleb sat on the floor with a truck and a race car. He looked up as they entered the room. Slade wanted to be a kid again, playing with cars and building forts.

Life was a lot easier then. But then, looking at Caleb, Slade wouldn't have missed this for anything. Even though he would have been okay with fewer hard times, more smooth sailing.

"I'm still hungry. But I ate cookies," Caleb confessed, even though the evidence was all over his face.

"Did you?" Slade opened the fridge door and pulled out butter and jelly. "Do you still have room for a sandwich?"

Caleb nodded and pushed the truck into the car, making a major crash. "Yep. And milk to drink."

"Milk it is." Slade grabbed the jug of milk.

Mia set a loaf of bread on the counter and then found the peanut butter and pulled out a skillet. "We could have something easier."

"I think I can handle buttering bread and spreading peanut butter and jelly on it." Slade found a knife and paper plates.

Making the sandwich was nothing compared to standing in Mia's kitchen, thinking about holding her again. He sure hadn't expected that to be the thought rolling through his mind as he buttered six slices of bread and stacked them on a paper plate.

Mia had moved away from him. She was sitting next to Caleb, showing him something with the truck. A moment later a battery-operated engine roared to life and Caleb shouted that it worked. Mia spoke softly to his son.

Slade spread peanut butter on three slices of bread and pretended that nothing in his world had changed in the past five minutes. But he knew he'd be lying to himself.

Chapter Five

Monday morning the alarm went off early. Mia started to hit snooze, but she knew that Slade would be showing up with Caleb. Jackson would be showing up, too, bringing the mare she needed to care for. She shook her head as she rolled out of bed. How did she get herself into these situations?

She dressed and then she walked down the hall to make tea. Before anyone showed up, she had plans. She brought her gun out of the gun cabinet. She left the ammo in the lockbox. No need to load the gun. She just wanted to see if she could make it work.

But it didn't work. She held the unloaded weapon in her right hand and eased it up, letting her hand rest on her left arm. Pain shot up her arm into her shoulder and she eased it back down. She wouldn't cry. The pain wouldn't make her cry. She tried to flex her fingers, praying they'd do what she commanded, but they wouldn't.

She picked up the weapon with her left hand and pretended to aim. She'd never been able to do more than scribble with her left hand. She'd always wished she had been born ambidextrous, like her brother, Travis. She wished it now more than ever.

Maybe if she worked at it long enough, she might be able to learn to shoot left-handed. She could teach her brain. She would make this work. Because without her job, what would she be?

That's the question she'd been asking herself for weeks. Who was she without her job? The DEA psychologist had made her write out a list. Sister. Daughter. Friend. Granddaughter to Myrna.

Sister to Breezy—if Breezy was still out there somewhere. She remembered her little sister, curly brown hair and dark hazel eyes. The day their mother died, the social workers had taken them all to Family Services. They'd been placed in a temporary home, together, until family could be found.

In the end, Mia had been the only one without biological family that could be traced. But she'd survived. God had given her the Coopers. She didn't regret. No regrets. Just sometimes emptiness, wondering about her little sister.

Breezy didn't seem to exist anymore. She wasn't on any social networking sites, not with her given name of Breezy. She didn't appear on any state websites. Which just meant she hadn't been in trouble with the law. No criminal record, anyway.

A truck with a rumbling diesel engine pulled into her driveway. Mia looked out the window. Slade's truck. She opened the front door and waited. He helped Caleb out and grabbed a bag from the back. The two walked up the sidewalk, Caleb in jeans, boots and a T-shirt. He pushed his straw cowboy hat back and smiled at her. Vicki's smile. It didn't hurt, not the way she expected.

Caleb was Vicki's son. He had her smile. He had her ability to make people look at the bright side.

Her gaze shifted up, to Caleb's daddy. No one else she knew could make that deputy's uniform look so good. Slade did it with a casual strength. His white cowboy hat tilted at a cocky angle and he pushed the brim up, flashing her a smile.

"Did you remember?"

"Of course I did."

"No, you didn't." Slade stepped up on the porch, holding a little backpack with a red car on the front, the other hand holding Caleb's. "We can do something else."

"Slade, I did remember and I'm ready. I even called Vera and asked for lunch to be delivered." She opened the door a little wider. "Come inside. What time do you have to be at work?"

"Soon." He stopped in the middle of the living room and then turned back to look at her.

Mia followed that accusing gaze and it landed on the weapon she'd left on the coffee table. Unloaded, of course. The bullets were locked in a cabinet in her closet.

"Slade, I had to try."

"Try?"

She moved her right arm, back in the sling since the failed attempt at holding her weapon. "I can't hold it. I can't pull the trigger."

His look changed, softened. She shook her head.

"I don't want sympathy." She picked up the weapon and smiled at Caleb. "Not for little boys to touch, Caleb. Ever."

He gave her a "duh" look. "I know that."

"I want to make sure. I wouldn't want you to get hurt."

"Mia." Slade's voice was soft.

"Slade, please stop. I'm good."

"You're always good, aren't you? You can conquer the world on your own, right? You don't need us mere mortals to lean on."

"I do. But I don't want to cry over it."

"You're more than this job."

She knew that. She had the list. Daughter. Sister. Granddaughter. "So I've been told. But could someone please tell me who I am?"

He smiled at her, an easy cowboy smile replacing the soft look of sympathy. He'd always had that easy charm. She thought about being seven, almost eight years old and attending church with the Coopers that first time. He'd smiled like that and told her he could beat her at tetherball. The challenge had pulled her out of her shell. How had he known it would work, just a boy of ten? How had he known her so well?

"Mia, you have to figure out who you are without the job. I can tell you who I think you are. You are the strongest woman I know. You're so strong you've never seemed to need any of us. You plow through life, taking on the world's problems."

"I'm not that strong." She'd just pretended and somehow managed to convince herself. "Let me put this gun back."

When she walked back into the living room, Slade was hanging the backpack on the hooks by her front door. She watched, unsure, really unsure. Slade turned, caught her watching. He shifted his attention to Caleb who had turned on the television to a kids' show with dinosaurs.

"Buddy, not too much TV, please, and make sure you're helpful."

Caleb nodded but kept watching the show. He had pulled a footstool close to the television and lay flopped over the top of it. His boots were on the floor next to him.

"He'll be fine, Slade. We'll be fine."

He indicated with a nod that she should follow him to the door. Mia glanced back at Caleb and followed Slade out the door.

"Mia, if this gets to be too much, I can call one of the ladies from church."

"It isn't too much. Stop worrying." She watched him frown, look away. "And we'll be safe."

"I know I'd be wasting my breath if I told you that you should stay with your parents until we figure out who broke in here and why."

"Yes, you wasted your breath. If I feel it's best, I'll go stay with them. Until then, I'm here and I'm figuring this out."

"Figuring it out? Mia, are you digging into something you shouldn't?"

"Maybe. Let me dig. Someone knew how to get here. We need to know who, or how they got that information. Right?"

"Right." His voice faded. "Stay safe and let me know what you find."

"I will. You're the only person I know I can trust right now."

"There are other people."

"Maybe, maybe not." She stepped close.

"You're right, you can always trust me."

"You be safe today, too."

And then he touched her cheek, the touch light and

fleeting before he turned and walked away. She watched his truck until it turned on the main road out of Dawson. And then another truck came up the road, this one pulling a trailer. Jackson. She opened the door and called for Caleb.

"Jackson is here with the horse."

Caleb let out a shout and then she heard his boots on the hardwood floor. He rounded the corner from the kitchen, happy the way a kid should be happy. She smiled. This was good, watching Caleb for Slade. For Vicki.

Mia closed her eyes for a brief moment and guilt replaced the moment of happiness. Slade had always been Vicki's. Friendship meant hands-off. She'd kept that rule since the day they were fourteen, when Vicki shared with her that someday she wanted to marry Slade McKennon.

She opened her eyes and smiled at her brother as he got out of his truck. Caleb ran out the front door.

"You like horses?" Mia asked, already knowing the answer.

He nodded but kept walking, his boots stomping on the wood slats of the porch. "My dad is letting me help him break a horse."

"Really? Breaking a horse at your age? That's pretty impressive."

He gave her a look, like it was no big deal and guys like him broke horses all the time. "I don't get on it yet."

"I see." She started down the steps and he followed. "I'll bet you're a good helper."

"My dad is the best. He can break any old horse."

"I know he can."

Caleb hurried to get to the trailer but slowed at the

end of the sidewalk to wait for her. "Did you know my dad is training a cuttin' horse for someone in Texas?"

"I think I'd heard that." She stopped next to the child. Jackson had a lead rope and was unlatching the back of the trailer.

"Hey, sis." Jackson stepped inside the trailer, the metal creaked. The horse whinnied and then shifted, restless from being inside.

"Jackson, I don't know if I can do this." She stepped close, peering inside.

"I know you can dump a can of grain and fill a water trough. That's what she needs now, that and some love."

"I might go back to work someday." The reminder might have been for Jackson, or for herself.

"Then I'll take her back to my place."

Mia stepped up on the side of the trailer and looked in at the mare. She was a bay, a deep brown with black mane and tail and black legs. And she was too thin. The mare turned her face in Mia's direction, revealing the warmest, saddest brown eyes she'd ever seen on a horse.

"Well, aren't you a pretty girl. Who leaves a sweet lady like you behind?"

Jackson now stood next to the mare. "Someone who runs out of options."

"Yeah, it happens." Mia rubbed the horse's velvety nose. "You are a fink, Jackson Cooper. You knew I'd love her."

"Been a long time since you stayed home and took care of a horse, Mia. You were the best."

"No, I just had the best behind me. And good horses."

Inside the shadowy trailer, the look on her brother's face changed. He went from easygoing to concerned, just like that, and Mia needed an out. She turned, motioning Caleb to join her. He stepped up on the running board and then the wheel well of the trailer. With five-year-old seriousness, he eyed the hungry mare.

"She's pretty thin."

"That she is, Caleb." Jackson spoke to the boy and then quietly to the horse that was having second thoughts about stepping backward off the trailer. The mare whinnied again. From somewhere in the distance another horse answered her fearful cry. Jackson continued to talk, convincing the horse she'd like her new home and she wouldn't be left again.

Mia shot him a look because the last was as much for her as it was the horse.

But maybe her brother was right. Maybe she wouldn't leave again. The injury might sideline her for good. And then what? People in town wanted a barrel-racing clinic for their kids. She thought back to when barrel-racing had been her first love. Her only love.

But she'd quit to pursue a degree in criminal justice, and then she'd taken a job with the DEA, eventually working on a task force that went after drug rings. Catching the dealers who poisoned children's lives had become her all-consuming love.

A thought whispered through her mind, that maybe she'd lost a little bit of who she had been in that dark world, lost herself to that job. A job shouldn't be a first love.

She had definitely lost her way.

Jackson handed her the lead rope of the mare. The horse stepped close. Caleb stood at Mia's side, his grin wide and his eyes bright as he stared up.

Maybe she and Caleb needed this mare as much as the horse needed them. Mia hoped she never had to admit that to Jackson. But from the knowing glint in his eyes, she guessed he already knew.

"What do we do now?" Caleb tugged on the hem of Mia's shirt.

"We put her in the field, give her feed and make sure the water trough is full. Can you help?" Mia handed him the tail end of the lead rope and positioned herself between the boy and the horse.

"I can help," Caleb announced. "Just wait until my dad sees her."

Mia let him help her lead the mare to the pasture. Jackson was there to unhook the gate for them. He also hooked up the hose for the water trough.

She let the mare go and watched as the horse grabbed a bite of grass and then moved on to another patch of green. The little boy next to her climbed up the fence to watch, his arms resting on the top rail.

"She sure is skinny." He shook his head as he made the announcement.

"We'll get her fattened up in no time, Caleb." Mia thought about how the words sounded like a promise that the horse would get better. But it also felt like a vow to be in his life for a while.

She didn't want to make promises like that, not unless she meant to stay in Dawson.

Slade didn't enjoy slow days at work, driving the country roads, with nothing but the occasional traffic violation, mostly speeding. But he also didn't like days like the one he'd just put behind him. He'd had a domestic call right off the bat, a battered wife who wouldn't press charges, and then he'd assisted Family Services in removing a child from a home. His day had ended with a car accident. He could never work an accident without remembering the night he'd driven up on the scene of Vicki's wreck.

As he pulled into Mia's driveway, he glanced at the clock on the dash. Almost eight o'clock. He rolled his shoulders to loosen the kinks before getting out. As he walked up the sidewalk the porch light came on and the door opened. Mia stepped out, holding her finger to her lips. He stopped and drew in a deep breath, because something held him for a minute. He took off his hat and swiped a hand through his hair.

"You okay?" she asked.

The soft voice reached through the twilight, and he hesitated. "Yeah, long day."

"Caleb's asleep. Why don't you come in and have something to eat?" Her voice remained gentle.

He stepped closer and the look in her eyes matched her voice. "Mia."

She took him by the hand and led him into the house. The living room glowed with the soft light of a floor lamp. The TV had been turned off. Caleb slept on the sofa, an afghan pulled up to his shoulders and his boots on the floor. Slade stopped to look at his son, at the peaceful expression on his face, the smudge of dirt on his cheek.

"He helped me with my new horse. We named her Sweet Lady. Kind of a long name, but he thought it had to be Sweet Lady, not just Lady. Any horse could be Lady."

Her voice held a smile as she spoke of her day with his son. He nodded and followed her into the kitchen. Lights blazed, music played, the volume low, and a candle burning on the counter smelled like cinnamon apples. His stomach growled and Mia laughed.

"Leftover fried chicken from Vera's." She took the leftovers out of the fridge, easing them onto the counter with her left hand, using her right to steady the container. "How's your mom doing today?"

"Has he worn you out already?" He moved around her in the kitchen, getting a glass out of the drainer next to the sink and a paper plate from the stack.

"Use real plates. And no, he hasn't worn me out. I love having him here. It's kind of hard to go from ninety to nothing the way I've had to do. I'd like to keep watching him, as long as you need me to."

"Thanks." He turned and she was behind him. A tomboy. She'd always been a tomboy. She'd never been the girl out chasing boys. She'd been the girl in shorts, T-shirts and boots hanging out at the arena, or hauling her horse to rodeos where she barrel-raced.

Tonight she looked different. Tonight she had a softer look in her eyes. If he didn't know better, he'd call her timid. That was the last word a man would ever use to describe Mia. If he said it out loud she'd take him down, even with one arm in a sling.

He'd had a long day. He'd seen too much, felt too much. And Mia was a friend. She'd always been a friend. And it had been a long time since he'd had someone to talk to at the end of a long day.

"Slade, are you okay?" She stepped a little closer and then her hand was on his. He lifted her hand, bringing her palm to his lips.

"Mia." He kissed her hand. It was the wrong thing to do. He knew it, but he couldn't stop.

He pulled her to him and held her tight because he needed her close. He needed someone to hold on to, just for a minute. Her head lowered to his shoulder, resting there for a few seconds.

When she looked up, he kissed her.

He drank her in, needing a moment with her in his

arms. She kissed him back. Her lips tasted like sweet tea and her skin smelled like lavender. He moved his hand to her waist, holding her close as his lips stilled on hers and he heard her whisper. She shook her head and he knew he'd stepped across a line that had always been between them.

"Slade," she whispered again and then she pulled herself out of his arms, away from him.

Common sense, reason and guilt hit him hard as he watched her back up to the counter, her fingers on her lips, her eyes wide. He brushed a hand across the top of his head and took a deep breath, exhaling with a whistle.

"Mia, I'm sorry." What kind of excuse could he give her? A long day? He'd had a long, difficult day? He had days when he was lonely, even surrounded by people?

If he said any of those things, he would hurt her worse than he already had. But for a moment, everything had felt right. He couldn't tell her that, either.

The few dates he'd been on in the past year hadn't been much to talk about. No one had moved him to make a second date.

No one had made him feel this guilty. He let the thought settle. Why did he feel guilty? Because kissing Mia had been different? Or because Mia had been Vicki's best friend?

Mia raised her hand, stopping him from making excuses and she didn't talk. Instead she turned to fix him a plate. He didn't speak, either, because she obviously didn't want him to say anything else. When she turned back around she held out a plate with a napkin over it.

"Start it at two minutes in the microwave. I'm going out to check on Sweet Lady."

"Mia…"

"No, Slade. I don't want you to say anything that

will make this more complicated. I need to think, and so do you."

"I know."

She stepped close again. "Do *not* say you're sorry, though. Because I don't know what *sorry* means right now."

With that she walked out the back door and into the night. He watched her go. He waited until the light came on in the barn and he could see her there with the mare. Only then did he take the plate she'd fixed him and heated it in the microwave. The windows were open and he could hear if anything went wrong in the barn.

He guessed something had already gone pretty wrong. How did he fix what they'd done? How did they go back to being friends? Did he even want to?

Slade and Caleb were gone when Mia came in from the barn. Slade had come out to tell her they were leaving and to ask if she was coming in. She'd told him she'd be in shortly. She watched his car drive down the road and she'd gone inside, locking the doors behind her.

She was sorry they'd left, sorry that her house no longer echoed with little-boy laughter, the sound of boots on hardwood floors or the crash of toy trucks. She stood in her kitchen and remembered a kiss.

If she closed her eyes, she could relive the moment. She could still smell Slade's cologne, the maleness of him. She could hear the way he'd whispered her name.

And she could feel the panic rise up as she realized what she'd done. It had been her fault. She'd taken the first step. Stupid. Stupid. Stupid.

How much could she complicate her life? She'd just found another way, by kissing Slade. She'd offered to watch his son. She'd fixed him dinner. She'd kissed him.

She tried to put it in perspective. She'd lost her job, her partner, the use of her right arm. Five years ago she'd lost her best friend, the one she'd always turned to when things went wrong.

Tonight Slade had just been a replacement, a stand-in for all that she'd lost. That had to be it. It made sense.

She poured herself a glass of tea and headed for the living room, still not believing the lies she'd just told herself. She wouldn't let herself examine it more. Not tonight, when she still felt emotionally bruised.

What she needed to do was work. She pulled out her computer and saw the box of photos she'd dug out of the closet, the lid still firmly in place. Pictures of her childhood. Pictures of Vicki. She set the box on the table but she didn't open it. Not tonight when she felt more than bruised—she felt guilty.

What she needed to do was focus on work. Work would keep her from thinking about other things. She had written a list while Caleb slept. Why would someone break into her house? What had gone wrong the day that Butch got shot? Who could have been the leak? She'd written down ideas and names. None of it made sense. Nolan had yelled something about the missing money. What money?

Butch wasn't dirty. She wouldn't let herself believe he had taken money. She knew that there were whispers in their unit, people talking, but she knew Butch. She knew how he felt about drug dealers.

Something had happened—she just didn't know what. She leaned back with her computer on her lap, replaying that day. Nolan had yelled about the money. She and Butch had been so close to tying everything up and putting that man away for years. Nolan's henchman, Ted, had come out of nowhere and yelled that they were cops and then he'd shot Butch. She'd shot Ted as he'd aimed at her. Nolan hadn't been armed and she'd held him until backup arrived.

She had it all written down, but maybe that was her mistake. What if someone broke in again and saw that she was working on the case? She took the papers to the kitchen and found a lighter. One by one she let them burn, holding them above the sink and then she sprayed water, washing it all down the drain.

Someone was dirty, but it wasn't Butch. She needed sleep, because it was all starting to run together and none of it made sense.

She checked to make sure all the doors were locked and carried her computer to her bedroom. Now to continue her search for Breezy. She'd found a website where she could post that she was looking for her sister. The website reunited separated siblings.

Mia pulled back the blankets and crawled into bed. "Okay, God, this is it. I can't let this go. There has to be a reason for that. Help me find her."

She looked around the quiet room with the overstuffed chair in the corner, the braided rugs on the floor and the wooden miniblinds closed tight. She knew that no one had heard her, other than God. No one had seen a lonely woman sitting in her bedroom talking to God.

After typing a message on a website to a sister she hadn't seen in about twenty years, Mia closed her computer. She needed to get some sleep. The lack of sleep could explain a lot of things.

Tomorrow would be a better day. She pushed the computer aside and sat propped against the pillows, staring at the black screen of the TV. She knew she wouldn't sleep. She hadn't slept in weeks. The pain, the dreams, reliving the moment in that dingy apartment, it all combined to keep her awake.

Tonight, if she did fall asleep, she feared her dreams would be as jumbled as her thoughts. She would dream of Butch, no doubt, the agony on his face as she held him, screaming for him to hold on. But she knew she would dream about Slade as well, about being in his arms and then feeling guilty.

Chapter Six

Slade pounded on the front door of Mia's house. It was eight o'clock in the morning. She never slept this late. She wasn't in the barn—he'd already checked. Her car was in the garage and she wasn't answering her phone.

"Where is she, Dad?"

"I'm not sure, Caleb." But he was sure of one thing. Mia wouldn't forget she was watching his son.

He pounded on the door again. He tried the knob again, just in case it wasn't locked, in case he'd been mistaken. He looked down at his son.

"Stand back, Cay."

"Got it, Dad. You want me to call 911?" He held up his emergency cell phone that he'd taken out of his bag.

Slade took a moment to grin. "No, I think I've got this. I'm a cop, remember?"

"Oh, yeah." Caleb backed up.

Slade took a good look at the door and slid a credit card out of his wallet. "I don't think I'll even have to break the door down."

He eased the card into the door that had probably been on the house for fifty years or longer and jiggled the handle. It worked and he made a mental note to get her locks changed. He pushed the door open and pointed for his son to stay put. Caleb frowned, but he'd stay where he was told.

Slade eased into the house. The urge to rush simmered and he walked quietly down the hall, checking each room. And then he got to her bedroom. The door was closed but not latched. He pushed it open, hand on his weapon.

"Mia?"

A lump on the bed moved, then bolted straight up, long hair cascading in all directions, covering her face. She was wearing the same clothes she'd worn the previous evening. Her computer was open on the bed next to her.

"What in the world are you doing in my house?"

He raised both hands in surrender, in case she was half asleep and had a gun hidden somewhere. "Checking on you. Obviously, you're fine. But I've been outside for thirty minutes. I've pounded on doors. I've checked your horse and called your phone. I didn't know I had Sleeping Beauty on my hands."

She reached for the cell phone on the side of the bed.

"Oh, Slade, I'm sorry. I didn't sleep much last night."

From the dark circles under her eyes, that was an understatement.

"When was the last time you slept, Mia?"

"Not open for discussion. Let me get cleaned up and I'll be out in a minute."

"I'll make you a cup of tea."

"Thanks.

First he let Caleb know that it was safe to come in. Then he headed for the kitchen and the cup of tea he'd promised to make. His phone rang. He answered and let the dispatcher know that he'd found Mia and he'd be hitting the road in fifteen minutes.

Mia walked through the door of the kitchen, a shy look on her face. He turned back to the hot water and the bag of tea—a lot easier to deal with than her.

"Mia, have you talked to anyone?"

"Talked? I talk all the time."

He held the cup of tea out to her. "You know what I mean. You need to sleep. You need to come to terms with this. It helps to talk."

"To a shrink. Just say it, Slade. Don't beat around the bush. You don't mean talk to you or Granny Myrna." She glanced at the clock and groaned. "She's going to be here in five minutes."

"You're babysitting Cay and she's babysitting you?" He grinned a little and she ignored it. He'd always been pretty convinced of his charm. Maybe he'd been wrong.

"She's helping me wash my hair." She turned a little pink at the admission.

"Mia, I'll go with you."

"To wash my hair?" She sipped the tea and reached in the cabinet for cookies. "Breakfast?"

"No, thanks, we ate at Vera's. That reminds me, there are biscuits and gravy in the car for you. Thirty minutes old but you can heat them up."

"I'd love biscuits and gravy."

"And a ride to Tulsa. I'm off tomorrow."

"I have a doctor's appointment tomorrow."

"In Tulsa? How convenient is that? Call your department and make an appointment to see the shrink."

"The only thing really boggling my mind right now that I might need counseling for is you. Why are you suddenly so involved in my life? Why can't you back off a little and let me have room to breathe?"

"Because we're friends."

She grimaced as she adjusted the sling around her neck. "I want this thing gone."

"And me?"

"Yes, I want you gone, too. But you make a decent cup of tea, you bring breakfast and you let Caleb play with me. I guess I'll figure out the rest."

"What time do we leave tomorrow?"

"Eight. Were you going to get those biscuits and gravy for me?"

"Yeah."

When he walked into the living room he stopped cold. Caleb looked up from the box he held on his lap. He had pictures spread out on the sofa and one in his hand.

"This is my mom, isn't it?"

Mia walked up behind Slade as Caleb asked the question, his blue eyes darting from the picture to Slade and then to Mia. Mia started to take the box and the pictures, but Caleb held them tight. Maybe this moment had to happen, for the child and for the father.

Hadn't he seen pictures of Vicki? Didn't Slade tell him the stories? She looked at Slade, waiting for him to unfreeze. He let out a long breath and then nodded.

"Yeah, buddy, that's your mom."

"Mia has lots of pictures and we just have that one on the dresser."

"Yeah, I know."

Mia sat down next to Caleb, sinking into the soft sofa, the pictures next to her moved and she reached for them. She picked one up and smiled.

"Caleb, this is your mom in high school. She was beautiful, wasn't she? And you look a lot like her."

The boy's nose wrinkled at that. "I'm not beautiful—I'm a boy."

Mia laughed. "You're right. Boys are handsome. And you are definitely handsome. But you have her hair, her eyes."

Caleb scooted close and looked at the picture. "Why was she dressed like that? All fancy and stuff."

"Your mom loved pretty clothes. I think this was a picture taken at a school dance. I think your dad was there with her. They were always together."

Mia's heart ached at the memories unfolding. She looked at Slade, saw the heartbreak in his eyes, saw it in the firm line of his usually smiling mouth. She smiled, wishing a smile could make this all better, make it hurt less. Why hadn't he shown Caleb pictures of Vicki?

"My grandma Bonnie says my mom was her princess."

Mia smiled, remembering Vicki's mom calling her that. Vicki's parents had moved to Arizona for Bill's lungs, but she knew they visited often.

"Yes, she was a princess. And she was my best friend."

"Really?" Caleb looked in awe. He found another picture, of Vicki on a horse.

The picture brought a rush of forgotten memories. "That was the day I taught her to ride."

"I need to call in." Slade spoke quietly, his voice steady.

"Why?" Caleb put the pictures down, suddenly nervous. "Dad, I didn't mean to."

"Caleb, you didn't do anything wrong." Slade rubbed a hand down his face. He squatted in front of his son and reached for the picture Caleb had put back in the box. "I'm going to call in and ask for today off so we can talk."

"All day?" Caleb's eyes scrunched as he studied his dad's face. "Are you sick?"

"No, kiddo, I'm not sick. But I think we need to talk and I don't want to leave right now."

Slade patted his son's leg and stood up.

Mia watched as he walked out the front door, already dialing his cell phone. She smiled at Caleb, who still looked worried.

"It really is okay, Caleb. Your dad loves you and he's not mad."

Caleb shrugged, but he stayed focused on the door his dad had walked out. They could hear the low rumble of Slade's voice and then the crunch of tires as a car pulled in the driveway.

"Look at this picture." Mia held up one of her favorites. "This is your mom at a youth group retreat."

"What's on her face?"

"Pie." Mia moved closer to Caleb and the little boy cuddled into her side. "We were on teams playing Bible trivia. Each time someone on our team missed an answer, your mom got a whipped cream pie in the face."

"Wow."

"Yeah, wow." She picked through the pictures looking for later ones. A picture of Vicki before her wedding, one of her holding Caleb.

The door opened as Caleb reached for the one of his mom holding him. Mia met Slade's dark gaze. She looked past him, to her grandmother. Myrna looked worried.

"I do love looking at old pictures." Myrna had a hand on Slade's arms. "It's good to hold on to memories. That's how we hold on to the people we loved."

Slade stood in the middle of the living room. He rubbed the back of his neck and watched Mia and Caleb. Myrna hurried around the living room, picking up a few things that were out of place, and if Mia knew her grandmother, thinking of a way to fix things.

"Mia, do you have one of those scrapbooking kits?" Myrna sat down on the edge of the chair across from the sofa.

"Gran, do I look like a scrapbooker? That would be your other granddaughter, Heather. She's the interior decorator, remember?"

"Right, you're not the crafter. You're the one who loved target practice with your brothers." Granny Myrna looked her over. "And a hairbrush wouldn't hurt you any."

Mia brushed her hand through her hair. "I didn't sleep."

"When do you sleep, Mia?" Granny Myrna pulled her chair closer to the pictures and picked one up. She smiled and handed it to Slade. "Look at that. Do you remember that day?"

Slade inhaled, his eyes closing briefly. "I think it was the Fourth of July. We went on a trail ride that morning and it was the first time Vicki had ridden for more than a few minutes."

Myrna chuckled at the memory they all shared. "She had to sit on a pillow."

Slade handed the picture back to his son. Mia stood and pointed to the spot on the couch she'd vacated. "Slade, you sit down with him."

"Can I make coffee first?"

"I can make it," Mia offered, already heading toward the kitchen. Slade caught up with her. "Go sit down."

"Give me a minute before I do this."

They were in the kitchen. From the living room she could hear her grandmother talking to Caleb, telling him stories, not just about Vicki, but about all of them. Slade was filling the coffeemaker with water. She knew avoidance when she saw it.

"Slade, you've had a minute. You've had five years of minutes." Her anger with him shook her.

"Don't, Mia. You don't get to barge into this part of my life the way you barge into everything else."

"*I barge?* You broke into my house. You insisted that I go to a shrink. *I barge?* I don't think so. I know that a child needs memories. I know that Caleb had a mother who loved him and you've let him live five years of his life as if she didn't exist."

He turned on the coffeemaker but he didn't turn to face her. His hands were palms-down on the countertop and he was leaning, looking out the window, ignoring her. Mia walked up behind him.

"I'm sorry," she whispered into his shoulder.

"I know. And so am I. Today I have to explain to my son why I haven't shared pictures and stories with him. I have to find a way to explain to a five-year-old boy that I missed his mom too much to let her memory into our lives. At first he was too little and he wouldn't have understood. Then he got older and I just didn't know how to bring it up."

He turned and she took a step back.

"Mia, it's been five years. I do talk about her, but…"

"I know. It's hard to move on."

"I'm moving on. I date. I raise my son. I've gone through the five stages of grief, probably more than once. And I'm here, I'm sane and stable and my son is good. But I didn't sit with him and share memories. I didn't show him pictures."

She looked away because she didn't know if she was ready for this. He'd been married to her best friend. How did she deal with his moving on? How would she feel if she saw him with someone else?

"It's okay for you to date. She would have wanted you to live your life. She would have wanted Caleb to have a family. She was an only child. She didn't want that for him."

"Right." He poured himself a cup of coffee. "I need to talk to Caleb."

"Granny and I will be down the hall if you need us."

"Thank you."

A few minutes later Mia walked into her bedroom, Granny Myrna right behind her. Mia reached around her grandmother and closed the door to give Slade and Caleb privacy.

"For a young woman who has kept herself pretty free from attachments, you're doing a mighty good job of making up for lost time." Granny Myrna walked past her, right to the bathroom. "Let's do something with that hair of yours."

"I should cut it all off."

"You should stop pretending you don't love Slade McKennon."

"I don't love Slade. We're friends. We've been friends for twenty years."

"You've loved him for eighteen."

Mia ignored her grandmother. She rummaged through the cabinet for a towel and shampoo.

"Gran, let's not do this."

Her grandmother wrapped a thin but strong arm around her waist. "Mia, I know love when I see it. You've always loved that boy. But you were a good friend. A loyal friend. I doubt anyone ever saw it but me.

Obviously, Slade never noticed. But men aren't known for their skills of observation."

"Please, let's just wash my hair."

"So you're going to continue to ignore your heart? You're going to pretend you're just a good friend who is willing to watch a little boy. You're as bad as that box of pictures."

"You're going to pretend you're not butting into my life." She said it with a smile because she couldn't really be angry with her grandmother.

"Of course I'm butting into your life. I have a beautiful ruby-and-diamond ring that belonged to my great aunt, a lovely Cherokee lady, the first of my ancestors born in Indian Territory. I want you to wear that ring someday."

"I can wear it today if you'd like."

"It will be your ring as soon as Slade can see what's as clear as that nose on his face."

"What does Slade have to do with my ring?"

Myrna hugged her in an easy hug. "Why, honey, do you really need for me to spell it out to you?"

"Gran, no." Mia shook her head. "Not me and Slade."

"Now, you tell me why not."

Mia pulled a stool up to the sink and sat down, hoping her grandmother would get the hint. Hair. Shampoo. Wash. Her grandmother didn't take hints. She stood there, arms crossed, lips pursed.

"Gran, he's Slade. He was the man Vicki loved." And Mia had kissed him just a day earlier. She remembered the kiss, how it had shaken her for so many reasons. She hadn't expected it to change things. She'd expected more guilt and less...whatever.

She groaned and closed her eyes.

"I guess you want me to wash your hair?"

Mia nodded her head and waited.

"Fine. But there's one thing you can do for that man you call a friend." Mia opened her eyes and waited. "Help him tell Caleb about his mama. Help him get past whatever he's holding on to."

"I'll do what I can."

When they'd finished, and walked back into the living room, Slade and Caleb were still sitting on the couch, still had the box of photographs between them. Mia's grandmother gathered up her purse and the light jacket she'd left hanging near the door.

"I think I'm going to go on home. Winston wanted to see a movie this evening and I think the early show would be better. I hate getting home in the middle of the night."

"Gran." Mia shook her head a little, but she knew her grandmother had a plan and she wasn't going to be convinced to stay.

"You're fine. If you need something, Slade can either take care of it or he can call me." Granny Myrna pulled a keychain out of her pocket. Attached to the keychain was a whistle and a small vial of pepper spray. That pepper spray always worried Mia.

"Slade doesn't have to take care of me." Mia walked her grandmother to the door. "I love you even if…"

"Even if I care so much I meddle?" Granny Myrna whispered close to her ear. And then she looked past Mia. "Slade, will you be riding that new horse of yours Friday night?"

Slade looked up from the box that sat between him and Caleb. "I hope to, Myrna. He's a little green but he should be fine."

"Well, you be careful, you hear? And Caleb, you enjoy those pictures."

With that she walked out the front door and down the sidewalk to her car. Mia watched until her grandmother was safely behind the wheel. *Safe* possibly being the wrong word for her grandmother behind the wheel. Finally, she turned to face what had to be faced. Slade and Caleb.

"Can I have copies of these for Caleb?" Slade asked, his voice gruff.

"Of course you can. I'll scan them and put them in an album with explanations, if you'd like."

"That would be good."

Caleb looked like a little boy with a lot of questions. Mia knew from her own experience how those questions piled up. She hadn't been much older than Caleb when a social worker, a stranger, brought her to Cooper Creek and left her with more strangers, telling her this was her new family. She had a new mom, a new dad and new brothers and sisters. She'd had a lot of questions. Fortunately, Angie Cooper had known without Mia asking.

"Cay, maybe we should head home." Slade started putting the photographs back in the box.

Caleb put his hand over the top of the box. "I thought Mia was watching me today."

Mia felt her heart get jittery. She was the last person Caleb needed to rely on, to attach himself to.

"I'm taking today off." Slade gently took the box from his son and finished putting the pictures away. The memories were too much, Mia thought. It felt as if Vicki had walked in on them.

Of course she hadn't. Mia shook off the ache in her heart. Or tried to.

"Are we going home?" Caleb looked like a kid trying to wrap his mind around what was happening in his always safe and secure world.

"Yeah, Cay, we're going home." Slade stood, tall and strong, always strong. Mia wanted to hug herself, protect herself from feeling things for him she shouldn't feel.

"Remember that I won't be able to watch Caleb after school tomorrow. I have a doctor's appointment in Tulsa."

"Oh, right. Mia, I'm off tomorrow. I planned on driving you."

"You don't have to do that."

"I want to. Caleb can stay with my sister. She's going to be driving up to help Mom clean her house."

"You're sure?"

"I offered, didn't I?" He set the box on the table and Caleb gave it a last, lingering look.

"Why don't you take those with you?" Mia picked up the box and held it out to Caleb. "I have more."

"Really?" Blue eyes lit up as he took the box from her hand.

"Really." Mia blinked quick and avoided looking at Slade. If she looked at Slade, she'd cry.

"Mia, I have pictures." Slade took the box from his son. "I put them away because I…"

He didn't finish. Caleb looked up at him, expecting him to say more, but a five-year-old didn't need hard lessons about grief. Slade met her gaze and Mia did her best to smile.

"I know." Mia reached for Caleb, wanting to hug him before he left. The little boy wrapped his arms around her waist and held her tight.

"I'll see you tomorrow morning." Slade grabbed his hat off the hook by the door on his way out.

"I'll be ready." Mia walked with them to the door, down the sidewalk to the truck. She stood there as they got in, buckled up, started the truck. Slade smiled at her and tipped his hat as he shifted and backed down her driveway.

Mia sat on her front porch after they left. There was little traffic but a couple of blocks away she heard trucks at the feed mill. In the distance she heard a tractor. It helped, to sit there and surround herself with what was familiar.

She thought about Caleb and Slade, working through their loss. Caleb would never know his mom. Slade had lost the love of his life. It had been five years, but sometimes grief came back without warning and shook a person all over again.

Being home she was learning something else. Old feelings that had been boxed up and put away, a little like those old photographs, sometimes returned. As an adult, the feelings were different and went past the old schoolgirl crush on the cute boy with the flirty grin.

As a woman, she saw the heart of the man he'd become. And she knew that he was good and kind, someone worth loving.

Could she even think about taking that next step—with him?

Chapter Seven

Mia pulled up to the Cooper ranch later that afternoon, proud of herself because she'd driven a stick shift left-handed. It had taken some talent to reach across and shift, but she'd managed. Her dad had just walked out of the barn and he shook his head, but grinned, as he headed her way.

She waited for him in the driveway.

It was always good to see Tim Cooper, also known as Dad. He had a steadiness that made her feel grounded. His quietness always reassured her. It had been that way from the beginning. She'd been his tomboy, the girl who loved to sit next to him in the enclosed cab of a tractor, the girl who would get on whatever horse he brought home. Her sisters, Heather and Sophie, both biological Coopers, not that it ever mattered to a Cooper, had interests other than the ranch.

Sophie, now married to Keeton West, helped to run Cooper Holdings. Heather lived in nearby Grove and had an interior decorating business. But lately she'd talked about moving to her section of Cooper land and building a house. Mia had land, too. She leased it to her brother Jackson. She hadn't needed it, not while she'd spent most of her time in Tulsa and other places she'd just as soon forget.

"Look who defied doctor's, and more important, her mother's, orders." Tim kissed her cheek. "Good to see you, Mia. You've been avoiding this old place, haven't you?"

"No." She smiled a little. "Well, maybe."

"So what brought you out today? Did you smell your mom's spaghetti sauce from three miles away?"

"No, but if I had, I'd have been here sooner." Mia slipped her left arm around his waist and leaned into him, loving that he smelled of horses, hay and fabric softener. Some things never changed, and she hoped they never would.

"I'm glad you're here. Jackson and Travis are in the barn trying to get a saddle on a gelding Travis bought at the auction. I'm not sure the animal hadn't been drugged before they took him in the arena."

"One of them will end up hurt."

"Wouldn't be the first time."

They had reached the house. Mia stopped because the lure of a horse that might be a little rank always got her attention. "I think I'll go on out to the barn."

"You'd better come in first, then you can go show the guys up."

"Okay." Mia walked through the door he opened for her.

Stepping into the house, she relived the day she'd been brought here as a foster child. She'd been over-whelmed by the size of the place, the number of people, the love. She'd felt like a scared kitten that everyone wanted to touch, pet. She'd wanted to find a corner and hide.

They'd let her hide at first. But they'd drawn her out

with their love. They'd drawn her into their family, making her one of them. She'd gotten used to the size of the house and then felt comforted by its warmth.

These walls were solid. The foundation was solid. As solid as the faith that guided the lives of the Coopers. And she loved them.

And yet, a part of her was missing. As she walked through the house, past family portraits and wall hangings made by various Cooper kids, she was aware of that missing piece of herself. Her sister, Breezy.

"Mia!" Her mom looked up from a cookbook open on the counter in front of her. She was wearing the apron she always wore, with handprints of all the kids when they were younger.

"I heard you were making spaghetti." Mia kissed Angie Cooper's cheek.

"I am, and if I'd known that was what it took to get you here, I would have made it days ago."

"It isn't the spaghetti, Mom."

"I know, sweetie." Angie touched her cheek. "Why the shadows under your eyes? Still not sleeping?"

Mia shrugged and considered avoiding the question. She was good at not answering. But her mom was more determined than most people. Mia could answer now or later, as Angie always said. It was her choice.

"I'm sleeping. A little."

"And worried a lot? About?"

"Where do you want me to start?"

Angie opened the fridge door and pulled out a pitcher of sweet tea. She poured three glasses and handed one to Mia. "Start at the beginning."

Mia sat down at the counter. Her mom sat next to her. Tim took his glass of tea and the newspaper on the counter and waved goodbye.

"So?" Angie patted her hand. This was a Cooper family ritual, sweet tea at the counter, Angie listening to whatever trouble had befallen her offspring.

They'd discussed love, lack of love, fights with friends and faith. All at this counter, sitting on these barstools. Mia remembered when Vicki died, sitting here with a box of tissues between them.

"Mom, I'm afraid I won't be able to work again. I'm worried about Tina. I feel as if I owe her something. I'm here and Butch isn't."

"Oh, Mia, you have to let go of that. You didn't do this. You tried to save him."

"He has a wife and kids. I'm single. He had someone waiting for him to come home."

"You have that, too, Mia. Every time you're gone, I worry nonstop about where you are and what's happening to you. I think of your being in danger, that I can't be there to protect you. I have to admit, sometimes I pray you can't go back to that life."

"I know." Mia choked on the words as emotion tightened her throat. "But Butch... I just...when I think of him... He asked me to make sure Tina was okay. I can't protect her because I don't know what she's hiding."

"Mia, if you think something is going on, you need to tell someone."

"But I don't know who to trust."

"Trust your instincts. Trust God."

Mia closed her eyes and shook her head. "I'm having a hard time trusting either right now. I felt that both let me down that day."

"God isn't going to let you down, Mia. He hasn't let you down. Life isn't always fair. It isn't always easy. Sometimes it hurts to be human. That's when you need God the most. Do you remember the illustration about the cross-stitch? The front is beautiful. The colorful threads design a picture or even a verse that we can frame and hang on the wall. But the back of the cross-stitch?"

"Knots, tangles, loose threads."

"Nothing beautiful about that, is there? But the finished product is a treasure. Life is a tangled mess, but God makes beauty out of that ugliness. We get past the hard times and we look back and see that He was there. The hardest times of our lives are the times when our faith grew the most, the times when He revealed himself in the most amazing ways."

"He made me a part of this family."

"You were a part of this family from the beginning, Mia. I will always believe that each child He brought to us, He knew from the beginning would be a Cooper." There was a short pause and then Angie patted her hand again. "So what else is bothering you?"

"Vicki."

"How's it going, watching Caleb for Slade?"

Mia lifted her glass of sweet tea, swirled the ice and tried to think of the best response. "Mom, Slade put away all of Vicki's pictures."

"I see."

"This morning Caleb found the box of pictures I'd brought out to look at."

"Oh."

"I just don't understand."

"We all face our grief the best we can, honey. Slade has managed to move on, to raise his son. Don't be too hard on him." Angie gave her a careful look. "Mia?"

Mia looked up from the glass of tea she'd been staring into. "Mom?"

"Is there more?"

Mia stood and walked to the sink. She poured the tea down the drain and rinsed the glass. "No, there's nothing else."

"If you change your mind, I'm here." Angie stood, loosening the apron and slipping it over her head. "Are you going out to the barn?"

"I think I will. Dad said the guys are having a hard time getting a saddle on a horse."

"Don't show them up too badly."

Mia's mood lightened at the thought. "I won't."

The newest stray at Cooper Creek joined Mia as she walked down the driveway to the barn. The big, husky-looking dog limped and one ear had a big tear. But he was sweet. Mia had been threatening to take him to her house, which her dad thought was a great idea. There were enough animals at Cooper Creek, he said, and it was about time she got a dog and stayed put in Dawson.

As she drew closer to the barn, which was really half stable and half indoor arena, she noticed a truck that hadn't been there when she first got to the ranch. She hesitated and considered turning tail and running. She'd never been a chicken. She'd never been a quitter. She wouldn't start now.

But then, she'd never had to face this much of herself, either. That was the thing about staying busy, it was easier to run from what you felt.

The big doors at the end of the stable were open. She could hear the guys talking, loud. She heard a horse whinny and then the obvious sound of hooves hitting wood. She picked up her pace and the dog at her side gave a low woof.

Inside the barn, the cause of the commotion was obvious. A big horse, dusky tan with a dark mane and tail, stood at an angle, ears back. He looked meaner than spit, but on second look, Mia saw him tremble and his dark eyes dart from man to man.

"What are you guys doing to that horse? You know better." Mia walked through the doors of the barn and two of her brothers, Jackson and Travis, plus Slade, turned to look at her. Standing a short distance away was Reese with his white cane held loosely in his hands. Dark glasses covered his sightless eyes.

"They think they're going to ride him today," Reese explained, taking a cautious step closer to the action.

"Since when do you break a horse by tossing a saddle on his back and bucking him out?" Mia ignored Slade and stopped next to Jackson. But if reasoning was going to be used, she'd have to turn to Reese.

"He was a saddle bronc, Mia," Travis explained, the bridle still in his hand and the saddle on the ground next to him.

"And you bought him, why?"

"He's pretty." Travis said it with a girly voice that did make her smile because of traces of his still-distinguishable Russian accent.

"Shut up." Mia walked around to the front of the frightened horse. "He's scared to death."

"I tried to tell them." Reese moved a little closer.

"I want him." Mia spoke softly as she stepped a little closer to the horse.

"Mia, this horse will get you hurt." Jackson cleared his throat. "I mean…"

"I might break an arm." She continued to speak softly, getting the horse's attention. "It's okay, Jackson, you can say it and I won't cry."

"I know, but…"

"But nothing, you guys have this poor horse scared to death. I want him."

"Mia, you can't break this horse. He's been rodeo stock for two years." Slade spoke with what he probably thought sounded like the voice of reason. To Mia, he sounded like a man who thought a woman needed his advice.

"Then what were you guys going to do with him?"

She glared at Slade. Her best glare, too. He didn't wither. She'd really hoped he would shrink back, show a little fear. Instead, he shifted into a more relaxed cowboy stance and pushed his hat up a smidge. She allowed herself one good look at the cowboy in his faded jeans and plaid shirt, pretending the look was one of dismissal, not approval.

He grinned and winked. "Care to take another look?"

"Okay, we're outta here." Jackson reached for Reese's arm. "I know that Maddie is going to be expecting me home soon and Cheyenne said Reese should help with the baby tonight so she can clean the shop."

Mia heard footsteps behind her. Travis escaping without a word.

Brothers. They were no help when a girl needed them.

So, this is how it went. Slade stood there watching the Cooper trio escape like little girls. And facing him was Mia. She ignored him in favor of the frightened buckskin gelding. She had a soft voice, a soft look. Her dark hair was pulled back in a ponytail and she must have planned this trip to the ranch. She wore a T-shirt, jeans and boots. She was the cowgirl he had grown up with, not the law enforcement officer she'd been since she graduated from college.

In the distance he could hear an old George Jones song playing on the radio. Travis preferred classic country to the new stuff. The horse snorted again and stomped.

"Mia, we have to get back to who we were."

She glanced at him but then turned her focus back on the horse. "Who we were when, Slade? Last year, or when we were kids?"

"We kissed, it isn't the end of the world."

She looked up, just briefly. "Oh, that."

She knew what he meant. She was playing with him. He wanted to… He watched her for a minute as she talked softly to the horse and then her hands were on the animal's face, gentle, soothing.

He wanted to kiss her again. Common sense jeered at him, called him a few names.

"Be careful," he said, not moving, just watching.

"I know what I'm doing." Her hand slid down the horse's neck. She was singing "Jesus Loves Me."

The horse trembled but his ears were no longer back. She stood at his side, still singing. "That's enough for today. Let's put him in his stall with a good memory."

She unclasped the lead rope from the ring on the wall and Slade opened the stall door. She eased the big horse around and he bolted into the safety of his stall. She took off the lead and stepped back, closing the door of the stall.

"Mia."

Slade didn't know what to say.

"Where's Caleb?" She walked away from the stall and he followed her down the aisle of the stable. She stopped at a door midway down and opened it. It led to the apartment that had once been Travis's.

"My sister came in earlier this afternoon. She said she wants him for the night."

"I see." She flipped on a light switch. "I don't want

to talk to my family right now. I don't want to deal with anything."

He followed her into the apartment. He'd crashed here a few times in his life. Coming home late from a rodeo, if he shared a ride with the Coopers, the guys would bunk at Travis's place.

She knew her way around the apartment. He guessed she'd stayed here a few times herself. His family farm didn't begin to compare to Cooper Creek. They ran a hundred head of cattle at the Circle M. They raised some good quarter horses and a few goats. He trained cutting horses for extra cash because being a county deputy wasn't going to do much more than pay the bills.

He'd built a house on the Circle M a few years ago. It was a decent house, big enough for two guys—himself and Caleb.

Mia put a cup of water in the microwave. They didn't talk. She leaned against the counter, sighing once. Ignoring him, definitely. In all the years he'd known her, they'd never had a moment like this. Their relationship had always been easy, comfortable.

Not that he had been blind. He'd always known she was beautiful. But she'd always been more like a little sister to him. It had been a code of sorts. A guy didn't mess with little sisters, even the gorgeous ones.

"Mia?"

"I've thought about selling my place and moving here, to this apartment." She opened the microwave, took out the cup of water, and dunked a tea bag in it. She continued without looking at him. "I don't know, maybe this would be too close to everyone."

"Maybe."

"Do you want coffee?" she offered. He shook his head. Together they walked through the apartment and out the back door to the small, privacy-fenced yard. They sat next to each other on a glider bench that rocked a little beneath their weight.

"When I think of the future, I think of Dawson. I don't even think about myself on the job. Tomorrow I should know more."

After her doctor's appointment.

"There's always…"

With a look she stopped him. "Do *not* say desk work. I'm a field officer. Undercover is what I do, Slade."

"I know. But it's a hard life."

"I think I know that better than anyone."

He sometimes wondered who she had been forced to become when she lived undercover. He wondered how undercover officers shrugged it off and went back to their real life, their real identity. If he had to guess, he would say with a lot of counseling and help from the people who loved them.

"Mom is making spaghetti. Do you want to stay for dinner?"

Her offer surprised him. But he couldn't stay. "I told my sister Eve that I'd bring home dinner from Vera's."

Silence again. Slade watched as Mia toyed with her cup, her thoughts somewhere other than there with him.

"What will you do?" he asked.

"Good question. I guess I'll say goodbye to a degree and a career. Maybe I'll raise a few horses."

"Settle down?"

"That's funny, Slade. What, me get married, cook pot roast and raise a few kids? You know me better than that."

"Yes, I know you." And even he could hear the change in his voice. She looked up, questions in her dark eyes, a spark of humor there, too.

She reached for his hand and lifted it, surprising him with a swift kiss on his knuckles. "Don't stop being my friend."

"I think you know I won't."

"I've never had a real relationship. When have I ever dated? High school, too busy with horses. College, too busy studying. After college? I guess I have a portfolio of on-the-job relationships, most of whom I could never bring home to meet the family." She laughed a little and he smiled. "I did date one agent who, I came to find out, had a hard time dealing with a female agent. He didn't like that I carried a gun and could shoot better than he did."

"His loss."

"Very true. Who wouldn't want a woman who could protect him in a tough situation?"

The mood had lightened and he breathed a little easier. "I know I'd be glad to have a woman who could keep me safe."

"I'm going to remember that." She pushed herself to her feet. "I should go up to the house."

He picked up her cup and followed her inside. A few minutes later they walked out of the now-quiet barn. The lights had all been dimmed.

Mia stopped at his truck. "The other day Caleb mentioned a party at school. He needs cupcakes."

"Thanks for reminding me. I tend to forget those things. I'll get some from the store."

Her hand rested on his arm and she stared at the ground, not at him. "I'll bake them. Or maybe I'll have mom bake them. My cooking skills are limited and more so right now."

"You don't have to do this."

"What, be a part of his life or bake the cupcakes? I

want both, Slade. I know I've been missing in action for a few years, but for now, I'm home. And if you want, I can go to the party, too."

"No, that's okay. I can drop the cupcakes off."

She sighed and her hand moved down his arm to his hand. Her fingers laced through his. "Slade, he asked me to go to the party."

"He asked you?" Slade needed a minute to process this.

"He wants someone at the party because the other kids have… Slade, I'm sorry."

"No, don't be. It's just that…" He didn't want to admit it, but sometimes grown men cried. Or at least teared up a little. And his son needing a mom at a school party had to be one of those moments. "Mia, I should have thought…"

Her hand squeezed his. "You can't think of everything, Slade. You're doing a great job with him. You're there in his life, loving him. He's a little boy and he sees everyone else at school, and…"

Slade took off his hat and drew in a deep breath. "I should go to the party. I should have thought about this."

"I don't mind going. I'd actually love to go."

"I don't want him to get the wrong idea."

"He won't. I'll make sure he knows that I'm doing this because I'm his friend."

He pulled the keys out of his pocket and opened the door of his truck. "For what it's worth, I'm glad you're home."

She stepped back and he got in the truck.

Friends. He tried to put her in that category as he drove away from the barn. She'd been his friend for years. Now she was Caleb's friend.

That ought to make him feel good, but when he tied

it together with the memory of kissing her, it just didn't quite match up.

Because he wanted to kiss her again.

Chapter Eight

Slade glanced at the clock on the dining room wall. Mia had called last night after he left Cooper Creek to tell him she'd meet him at his place this morning. To make it easier.

"Caleb, buddy, the bus is going to be here soon." Slade buttoned his shirt as he walked down the hall. He peeked in Caleb's room. "What are you doing?"

"I gotta take something to school for show-and-tell." Caleb slipped something in his pocket but his cheeks turned red and his blue eyes darted, not making contact.

"What have you got in there, a lizard or something?"

Caleb shook his head fast and grabbed his backpack. "The bus is going to be here."

"Right. And you aren't going anywhere until you tell me what's going on."

"Mia's going to be here."

"Caleb, hand it over. I'll have Aunt Eve take you to school if you don't 'fess up now."

He glanced at his watch. They had ten minutes before the bus got there.

Caleb put his hand in his pocket and pulled out a photograph. Slade didn't have to see it to know who was in the picture. He sat down on the bed next to his son and Caleb handed it over with a frown.

"Show-and-tell, Caleb?"

"One of the kids said I didn't have a mom. That I hatched from an egg."

"Who said that?" Somehow he kept his voice from shaking as his temper spiked. He didn't know if he was mad at some kid or mad at himself for messing things up.

"I don't want to get him in trouble." Caleb's voice wobbled. He didn't look at Slade. He sat on the bed and rubbed his finger over the red car on his backpack.

"Okay, don't tell me who. But you had a mom and she loved you a lot, Cay. You were everything to her, to us."

"I guess."

But he wanted to be like the other kids, with more than pictures. Slade got that. Vicki had been gone before Caleb could even have memories. Slade wrapped an arm around his son and held him tight.

"You take the picture to school if that's what you need to do. But promise me you'll talk to me next time. Anytime you have questions about anything, I'm here." He didn't want his son to think he had to hide things. But he kind of guessed he hadn't been an open book. "Cay, I'm sorry if I've let you down."

Caleb looked up, his blue eyes intent, but he didn't say anything. Slade held out the picture and his son took it and shoved it into the small pocket on the front of the backpack.

"Remember, I won't be here when you get home."

Caleb nodded. "'Cause you're going to the doctor with Mia. Is she okay?"

"Yes, she's good. And when you have the party at

school, she's going to be there and bring cupcakes." There, he'd said it and now he couldn't back out.

"Cool!" Caleb jumped up, then turned quick to hug Slade. "Thanks, Dad. The guys will think it's cool because she has a gun and got shot!"

"Whoa, Caleb, that's not exactly the way you need to introduce Mia, okay? She isn't something you bring to show-and-tell."

"But she's cool."

"Yeah, she's cool but I don't think she wants you to talk about what happened to her."

"Okay, I won't."

"Thank you." Slade cleared his throat. "I hear the bus."

He followed Caleb down the hall to the front door. The bus stopped at the end of the drive. Caleb ran out, backpack flapping against his side. He stopped at the edge of the drive, waved and then climbed the steps of the big yellow bus. He was in kindergarten. When had that happened? Slade stood in the door, watching until the bus disappeared from sight. Still no sign of Mia.

He walked back into the house, needing a few minutes to finish getting ready. In his room, his gaze landed on the one picture of Vicki he hadn't boxed up—their wedding picture. He picked it up, staring into the open face of a woman who had kept him smiling. She'd been nineteen, he'd been almost twenty-one when they said their "I dos."

Mia had been the one and only bridesmaid. Reese had been his best man.

A truck came down the road. He spotted it through the open curtains. Mia's truck. He walked into the bathroom and ran a washcloth over his face to get rid of the last of the shaving cream he hadn't washed off before he'd had to get Caleb moving.

"Anyone here?" Mia's voice, muffled by walls.

"Be there in a second."

He splashed aftershave on his cheeks, wincing when it hit a nick. He found Mia in the dining room, standing in front of the French doors that looked out on the back deck he'd never really done much with. No shrubs, no flowers and only a few folding chairs.

"You could use some patio furniture out there."

"Yeah, one of the things I never get around to." He poured coffee into a travel mug. Mia moved away from the door. She was wearing a long skirt that swished around tanned legs and a dark blue top that fell to her hips. He took a sip of coffee and looked away.

"I have to go by the field office."

He picked up his keys and cell phone. "No problem."

"They have questions about Butch, about Nolan Jacobs's claim that money is missing."

"Mia, this is going to work out. They'll figure out who took it."

"I hope so."

They walked out the front door and he locked it behind them. He hadn't always locked the doors but with the economy the way it was, sometimes people got desperate. He'd been on too many calls lately to be careless.

"I can drive my truck," he offered.

"No, drive mine. It needs to be driven and I filled up the gas tank on the way over."

He opened the passenger-side door for her. She gave him a look but got in with a quiet "Thank you" and no real grief over his being a gentleman. If she said anything, he'd have to tell her that he'd open the door every time because he was more scared of his mother than he was of her.

They drove in silence for a long time. Mia had closed her eyes. Slade turned the radio to a country station that played more music, less news. Or so they said. The first song out was something by Keith Urban. A new song about being willing to give up his life for the one he loved.

"Turn it off." Mia spoke into the quiet, only the radio playing.

Slade agreed, turned off the station. The words to the song probably brought up too many memories for both of them.

"I'm sorry," she said, her voice still soft.

"I get it." He glanced her way and reached for her hand.

An hour later they were pulling into the parking lot of the medical clinic. Mia sighed and reached for her fringed purse.

"I can take it from here."

"I'm going in with you." Slade pulled the keys out of the ignition. "Did you think I meant to drive you into town and drop you off?"

"I don't know."

They met at the front of the truck. Slade had left his white hat in the truck. He brushed his hand through his hair, smoothing the ridges left by the hat. Mia smiled up at him.

"You look fine."

He could have told her the same thing. He didn't.

"I told Caleb this morning—" he walked next to her "—that you're going to the party with him. I told him you'd be there."

"Oh."

They stopped at the doors of the clinic. An older man walked out, pushing his wife in a wheelchair. The wife smiled and waved at them.

"Honeymoon accident." The woman giggled and indicated her casted foot.

Slade smiled at the lady and her announcement.

"Um, congratulations?" Mia smiled at the couple and the husband winked.

"Been married a month. She slipped on the deck of our sailboat."

The conversation ended, the newlyweds continued toward a sedan in the handicapped parking space. Mia looked at Slade and he had to laugh.

"Sometimes lightning strikes twice," he offered.

"I've heard if a person is hit once, they're more likely to get hit again."

"I don't know." And then they were at the reception window and he had serious doubts. He'd loved Vicki with his whole being. How could he love that way again when he'd already given all of his heart to the woman he thought he'd spend his life with? How did a guy get that lucky twice?

Mia walked out of the doctor's office an hour later with a sling, no splint and an arm that was pale and starting to atrophy from lack of use. Slade stood when she walked through the doors of the waiting room.

"How's it feel?"

She wiggled her fingers and blinked when tears stung her eyes. "Let's go."

"Okay." His hand touched her back and he guided her from the building into bright September sunshine. "Mia?"

"I can't talk." She walked away from him, wiping at her eyes, angry with herself for crying.

"Mia."

Slade walked up behind her, catching her and holding her tight against the solid wall of his chest. She turned into his embrace and his arms circled her, strong, reassuring, comforting. That might have made her angry, too, that she needed comforting.

She wanted to stomp her foot and get mad at the situation, not give in to it.

She didn't cry, though. She rested her cheek on the soft cotton of his shirt, heard his steady heartbeat close to her ear. And called herself a cheat.

She backed out of his embrace. "I'm fine."

"Of course you are. You're Mia and you're always fine."

"When have you ever known me to not be fine?"

"Well, if we're being honest…"

"Stop. I'm fine."

"What did the doctor say?"

"Well, for starters, I'm probably going to have to get a truck that's an automatic because I'm not going to be able to shift." She swallowed fast as tears threatened again. "And I'll probably need to perfect this left-handedness."

"I see." He opened the truck door.

She climbed in and reached across to grab the seat belt and when she tried to shove it in the buckle the tears released. "I can't…"

"Let me."

"No."

She shoved it into the buckle as Slade held the metal steady.

"You can let me help you. Tell me what the doctor said."

"The nerve damage is severe. With time and physical therapy, maybe more surgery, I'll regain some strength and mobility." She repeated what she'd been told and looked away, at the city that had been her home away from home for the past few years.

"That's a start. And I know you. You're going to fight this."

"I'm so tired."

"I know."

She closed her eyes and shook her head. "I haven't slept in weeks. When it wasn't hurting, I was having nightmares."

"We'll have to fix that."

"How?" She looked at him, waiting for some brilliant suggestion. She thought of some sarcastic replies that even she wouldn't appreciate.

"I'll think of something."

"Okay, so now we have to go to the office. I'm not ready for this. I'm exhausted."

"When we're finished we'll get lunch."

She nodded, but she didn't want to think about lunch, about the interview or about the counseling session.

A short drive later they parked and got out of the truck again. Mia approached Slade slowly, afraid of being weak and needing him, afraid she was confusing her emotions. Maybe she did need counseling.

Once upon a time, they'd both been young, free from scars, thinking the world couldn't hurt them. They stood facing each other now and she wanted to touch the fine lines at the corners of his eyes that crinkled when he smiled. She wanted to trace her fingers through the subtle gray in his hair.

She had a strange urge to put her hand on his heart, to know if it beat unevenly when broken. She turned and headed toward the office.

"I'm not sure how long this will take." They were in the elevator going up.

"It's okay."

"You don't have to wait here."

"I don't mind. I'm sure they have somewhere I can wait."

The elevator doors opened. Tina stood there, one of her two children close to her side, her pregnant belly very obvious in the light yellow sundress. She was young and pretty. Her smile dissolved when she saw Mia.

"Tina, how are you?"

Tina looked down at the little boy who was probably too young to know what was happening. "I'm good. I had to come in. They're asking a lot of questions. Mia, I don't know what to tell them."

"The truth, Tina."

"I told them everything I know." Her hand rested on her belly. "I have to go."

"Do you have family here to help you when the baby comes?"

Tina shook her head. "No, but I'm good."

"I can be here for you. Please, I want to be here."

Tina touched her arm. "Mia, it wasn't your fault."

Mia couldn't respond to that. She struggled every day, feeling guilty for being alive, guilty for not acting faster. If she could have saved Butch…

"Mia, Butch wouldn't want you to feel this way."

"But I do. And I want to be there for you. Anything at all, just let me know."

"Okay, I will."

A door opened. She glanced to the right, saw her supervisor and he wasn't smiling. "I have to go. But, Tina, I'll call you. If you need anything, I'm here."

Mia left Slade and walked down the hall to her supervisor's office. He motioned her in, not smiling, not giving anything away. Dread tightened as if a clamp had been attached to her heart, to her lungs.

"Mia, take a seat."

She did.

"How's the arm?"

She shrugged. "It's been better."

"And you?"

"I'm getting better, too. I'm not sure if I can come back. Jay, I'm not sure."

"Mia, take your time. We need to discuss how this operation got compromised. Did you ever leave the op and meet with a civilian?"

She shook her head. "No, why?"

"Mia, did you know that Butch had met with Tina?"

She closed her eyes and shook her head again. Her temples throbbed and she wished she could escape all this. "No. He wouldn't have."

"He did. We're doing a full investigation, but we're having a hard time finding our guy on the inside. We think he has the money and somehow made it look like Butch took the cash," her supervisor explained.

The man he spoke of, the one on the inside, had been one of Nolan Jacobs's men they'd baited and caught. They'd been using him for information.

"We knew he was a liability from the beginning." Mia hadn't trusted the whole situation.

"Mia, I want to know if you remember anything. And if you need anything, we're here."

She nodded and stood. "I've got an appointment."

"With Dr. Kim? I know this hasn't been easy. We're all hoping you can get back to us."

"Thank you."

She walked out, his parting words were for her to be safe and to let him know if she thought of anything.

But who could she trust? If someone on the inside was involved, how did she know who to talk to if she thought of anything?

Slade. She saw him at the end of the hall and she knew that she could always trust Slade. She checked the time and headed his way. "It will be another hour. You really can leave."

"Mia, I'll be here."

"Good." She smiled, wishing for an easy gesture. "I guess I'll see you when I'm done."

She walked away, knowing that she needed this counseling session. She wanted to be herself again, the old Mia who conquered. She wanted to be the friend Slade called from time to time just to say "hi" and see how she was doing.

She would get back to being the person she'd been. The person who'd had faith. Faith. She stopped at the door to the counselor's office. She could hear her mom telling her to have faith and that God would do something with this situation.

She had never been good at waiting. Maybe He was using this to teach her how to wait for Him? Because if she waited, she remembered the verse, He would renew her strength.

Chapter Nine

Slade glanced at the woman sitting in his truck as they drove toward Dawson. She'd been quiet since the counseling session. During lunch she'd picked at her food and he hadn't questioned her.

"Stop looking at me." She had her eyes closed and her head back.

"I'm not."

"You are. Quick glances. See, you did it again."

He laughed. It felt good to laugh. It eased a lot of the tension that had been building between them. She opened her eyes and smiled at him. He looked away, back to the road. *Focus on the road.* He'd forgotten how beautiful she looked when she smiled that way.

"Okay, I looked at you. I've been wondering how you feel," he admitted.

"I'm tired but maybe I'm getting to the other side of this."

"Of course you are."

"Tina met with Butch while we were working undercover. They think he got followed. Why did he take that chance, Slade?" She turned slightly in her seat to face him. She drew up her legs, pulling the skirt around them and tucking it.

He cleared his throat and concentrated on the long drive to Dawson.

"Because he missed her. They spent a lot of time apart. She was probably just finding out she was pregnant when the two of you left. And she had to deal with the fact that he spent more time playing your husband than actually being hers."

"I know." Mia looked straight ahead. "I sometimes think that's why she isn't willing to talk to me."

"She's working through a lot. Probably some of her own guilt." He eased into the passing lane to get around ld farm truck hauling too many round bales. "How ounseling session go?"

"Same old, same old. She asked me to think about who I am without this job. She wants me to visualize my life without it, because that's a good possibility. And she asked me if I might be dealing with depression."

"And?"

"I'm not depressed. I can't sleep. End of story."

"Depression isn't incurable, Mia. It isn't a sign of weakness."

"You think I'm depressed?"

"I'm saying you've been through a lot and sometimes when we suffer trauma like you've suffered, it happens."

"I see. You sound like a man who knows."

"I'm a man who needed help after my wife died. I fought it. I didn't want to feel weak. I didn't want to feel as if I wasn't trusting God."

"I see."

"I had to face the fact that I needed help. I had to get my life back. I did it so I wouldn't let Caleb down."

"Slade?" Her voice sounded sleepy.

"Yeah?"

"Thank you. For sharing that."

"We're friends." He kept on driving while she fell asleep.

She hadn't slept in a while, not really. He thought about taking her home, but that would mean waking her up. And then when would she sleep again? He checked the gas gauge. He had filled it up before they left Tulsa so he had a few hundred miles to burn before it got close to empty.

That meant several hours of driving time. He picked up his phone and dialed his sister.

"Hey, is everything okay?" Eve asked. She was the sibling he always counted on. His two younger brothers were usually off chasing the next bull-riding event or a female who didn't want to get caught.

"Yeah, good. Listen, is Caleb doing okay?"

"He's having a blast. We made cookies. Now we're going to town."

"Can you hang on to him a while longer?"

She hesitated. "Sure, why?"

"I'm driving, Mia is sleeping. She needs to sleep."

Another long hesitation. "So you're going to drive?"

"If that's what it takes."

"Slade, is there something…"

He cut her off. "This is what you do for a friend."

"Right. Okay. Call me later."

He told her goodbye and he kept driving. After a couple of hours of the radio and Mia's soft breathing, he took the back road and headed into Dawson. Mia slept on. Once he thought she might be about to wake up. She cried out in her sleep, moving next to him. He touched her hand, covering it with his, holding on until she quieted.

Eventually, he parked in the back lot behind the Convenience Counts convenience store on the edge of Dawson. Tricia, owner and manager, stepped out. When she saw that it was him, she waved and fortunately left well enough alone. Explaining to Tricia was the last thing he wanted to do, especially since he couldn't explain to himself what he was doing.

Helping a friend sounded easy, uncomplicated. He'd enjoyed his life being uncomplicated, just him and Caleb, and an occasional date that went nowhere. When he looked at Mia, he saw a complication. The list of reasons was long.

How did he get involved with the best friend of the wife he had loved and lost? How did he get involved with someone who had a career that might take her back undercover and away from them for months at a time, especially when Caleb had gotten so attached to her?

He sat there watching her sleep. The other thing he couldn't stop thinking about were his recent prayers asking God to help him move on.

The sun had set behind the building, leaving the back parking lot in shadows. Slade moved in the seat and put an arm around Mia. She moaned in her sleep but she relaxed and leaned against his shoulder. He kissed the top of her head and leaned back, holding her easily against him. She breathed in deeply, then exhaled and sighed.

Mia awoke with a start. It was nearly dark. She didn't know where she was. An arm held her loosely, circling her shoulder, keeping her close. She blinked a few times and turned to look into gray eyes that watched her intently. She raised her hand and rested it on his heart. The beat was steady, sure.

"What time is it?" She looked around, at the twilight sky. "Shouldn't we have been home a long time ago?"

"I let you sleep."

She moved and he sat up. "Let me sleep?"

"I drove—" he looked at his watch "—for a few hours. You needed sleep, Mia."

"How long have we been sitting here?"

He laughed a little, and she had the good sense to feel nervous. "Long enough for everyone in Dawson to spread the story."

"That's bad." She leaned into him again, resting her head on his shoulder. "We should go."

But she didn't want to. Leaning against Slade had to be the most comfortable place she'd ever been, the most restful. Slade felt like home. And home always felt safe, like a sanctuary from the real world.

"Your grandmother parked behind us for a few minutes. She looked like she might get out and do a happy dance. I guess I should have kept driving, but I didn't want to run out of gas."

Mia rubbed her hands over her face and blinked sleep from her eyes. "Gran catching us could be bad. But I feel better than I have in weeks."

"Are you hungry?"

"Starving."

"Vera's closed. Do you want a slice of pizza or a corn dog from the convenience store?"

"Why not?"

She watched him go inside and then she pulled the keys from the ignition and stepped out of the truck. It was a beautiful night. The air was crisp and smelled like the country, like cattle and grain from the mill and fried food inside the store. Millions of stars twinkled in the velvety sky. Somewhere a radio played, but she couldn't make out the song. She let the tailgate down on the truck and took a seat.

A few minutes later Slade sat down next to her. He put two bottles of water between them and handed her a corn dog and a packet of mustard. She took it. She'd never been a fan of corn dogs but at that moment, sitting on the tailgate of her truck, rested for the first time in weeks, it was the best meal she'd had. Maybe ever.

"Are you going to the rodeo Friday?" Slade asked after he finished scarfing down his corn dog. Mia looked at him, finding the question funny for some reason. Maybe because she'd slept and she felt good. Maybe because it took her back to the old days.

"I plan on it."

"Caleb wants to ride his pony in the kids' pole-bending event. I don't know if he's ready."

"Of course he is. Even if he doesn't win, he's ready."

Slade looked down at her, an easy smile on his face. "I really am glad you're back."

"Me, too. And I'm glad you're still my friend."

"Haven't I always been?"

"Yes, you have." She leaned, touching her shoulder to his. "I haven't been the best friend I could have been."

"You've always been here for me. Maybe not in Dawson, but if I needed you, I knew where to find you."

"Slade?"

"Mia?"

"I'm scared."

"I know."

She moved out of the circle of his arms and looked up at the sky. "We should go."

"Probably a good idea." He hopped down and reached for her hand, helping her down from the tailgate as if she was someone else, someone who needed chivalry and moonlight.

She took his hand and he led her to the cab of the truck, opening the door for her and helping her buckle the seat belt. She leaned back, letting him offer his help, grateful for it.

It had taken this accident to teach her to let people help her. She told him that, and he smiled and closed the truck door. It had taken this accident to bring her home. She watched Slade in the side mirror. She watched him put up the truck's tailgate. She watched him take a minute to look up at the stars. When he came to get back in the truck, she pretended she hadn't been watching him.

"How about I take you to your house and I'll have Eve bring your truck in tomorrow?"

"That's too much trouble."

"No, it isn't." He turned down the road to her house. "Mia, I don't want you to drive home alone. I don't want you to go in your house alone."

"That's sweet, Slade, but I'm really okay. I do know how to take care of myself."

He parked her truck in front of her house, obviously not letting her make the decision this time.

"And I know that no matter how prepared we are, things happen."

"You're going in with me, aren't you?"

"I plan on it."

She reached to push her door open. "Suit yourself, cowboy."

He followed her up the sidewalk to the front door and she handed him the key.

Slade opened the door and flipped on a light switch. Mia thought about yelling, "Boo" but then thought better of it. He probably wouldn't appreciate her humor at the moment.

"Are you going to check out the whole house?"

"I planned on it." He walked through the house, flipping on lights, checking closets.

Mia waited in the kitchen. She needed to look in on the mare. When he came back from his security check, she handed him a glass of tea.

"I have to make sure the mare has water."

"I'll walk with you." He set the tea on the counter and she stopped him, placing her hand on his arm.

"Slade, I've got this. I'm going to walk out there and check on my mare. You're going to drink your tea." She patted his arm. "And then you're going to go home and take care of Caleb."

He opened his mouth to object. She shook her head, stopping him.

"You've been a great friend today. And I needed a friend. I definitely didn't need family. I love them, but they want to do everything for me. They want to fix me. You made this day easier."

"Thank you. Or should I say, you're welcome?"

"Both." The smile came easier now. Maybe life wasn't back to normal, but she felt a little more like herself. She kissed him on the cheek. "If I'm not back in five minutes, send out the posse."

"Got it."

The mare was waiting for her. The pretty bay stuck her head over the fence and Mia ran her hand down the horse's sleek neck. The animal already looked better. Maybe she just looked happier, because she had a home again.

Mia lifted the handle of the water spigot and the hose gurgled and then spurted as water poured into the trough. The horse took a long drink and then looked around, water dripping from her mouth. Mia turned, too, the hair on the back of her neck standing.

With the light on the back porch, she couldn't see into the dark. Chills ran down her arms and she tried to reach for a weapon that wasn't there.

With easy movements she pushed down the handle on the spigot and petted the horse one last time. She started toward the house, waving at Slade. He waved back. She was fine. It had been a case of nerves, nothing else.

Slade opened the door. "How's the horse?"

"Good." She walked past him to the sink and washed her hands.

"Mia?" He looked at her and glanced out the door. Without asking he clicked the lock in place and then the dead bolt. "What happened?"

"Nothing."

"Nothing? I'm not buying that."

"Seriously, nothing happened. I just got spooked." She hooked an arm through his and walked him out of the kitchen. "I'm good. You can go."

"I'm supposed to leave and you're going to do what?"

"I've been taking care of myself for a long time."

"You drive me crazy, you know that?"

"Yes, I probably do." She stopped at the door with him. "I got spooked, Slade. There's a lot going on and one thing I do have is an overactive imagination. So go home and try to relax."

"Let me take you out to the ranch."

"I'm not going to the ranch because I've got a case of the heebie-jeebies."

"Fine, I'm staying."

"That would start more than a few rumors and result in a shotgun wedding with my grandmother holding the shotgun."

He drew in a deep breath. "All right, I'm going. But I'm calling county and telling them to drive by here tonight."

"You do that." She walked out the front door with him. "You can pray for me, too."

"I'm glad you'll let me do that." He brushed a hand across her cheek.

For a second she thought he would kiss her. But he didn't. And for much longer than a second, she was disappointed, filled with regret, then guilt.

Chapter Ten

Mia stood next to Travis as he unloaded the gelding she had asked to borrow for the Friday-night rodeo. The horse, a pretty roan, backed out of the trailer without a halter, not seeming to care what was going on around them. She liked that about him.

"You're sure about this?" Travis handed over the lead rope.

"Why wouldn't I be? Come on, you're the one who offered the horse."

"Right, and I'm the guy in trouble if you get hurt."

"I take full responsibility."

She led the horse around the trailer and tied him. His dark gray tail swished. Travis pulled the saddle, pad and bridle out of the trailer.

"There you go." Travis stood behind her, hands behind his back, hat pulled low. "Elizabeth is heading this way to try to talk you out of this."

"I can handle her."

"Right." He grinned that cute grin of his that had gotten him in a lot of trouble over the years, until Elizabeth came along. "Let me saddle him for you."

"I can do it. You go do what you need to do."

"I'm going to saddle my horse after I buy my pretty wife a burger."

Elizabeth walked up, with a baby bump and a soft glow on her face. "You're really going to do this?"

"I have one good arm and a great horse."

Elizabeth looked the horse over. She had learned to ride, but admitted that it wasn't her favorite hobby. She still made trips to St. Louis to help with the family business, although those trips had stopped with the baby on the way.

"Just be careful."

Mia smiled at her sister-in-law. "I'll be careful."

Travis put an arm around his wife's waist. "Buy you dinner, Mrs. Cooper?"

"Yum, rodeo fare, my favorite." She wrinkled her nose and laughed.

But she hooked her arm around Travis's and off they went, an unlikely couple. Mia watched them for a minute, smiling and then feeling strangely sad. Maybe because lately everyone she knew had turned into a couple. Except Heather. At least Heather was still single. And possibly moving closer to home so they could see each other more often. Not that Grove was that far from Dawson, just fifteen minutes.

Mia had never seen herself as half of a couple. She'd been pretty content with her career. She'd been married to it, she guessed. And now? Divorced from it. The thought ached deep down because she was starting to face the loss.

She picked up the saddle pad and eased it into place on the back of the roan gelding. The saddle would be more difficult—she knew that. Her left arm had gotten stronger because she had relied on it for the past couple of months, but her brain refused to believe she was now left-handed.

She lifted the saddle and eased her weak right arm under the leather skirt. Pain shot through her arm into her shoulder. She took a deep breath and lifted, putting the pressure on her left arm. But she couldn't get it high enough. The horse moved away from her, pulling the lead rope loose. She set the saddle down and tightened the rope.

"What are you doing?"

She didn't turn around. She had known Slade would be here, but she didn't want to look at him, not now when she felt weak. Weak in so many ways she hadn't expected.

"I'm going to ride tonight."

"Barrels? Mia, is that…"

She spun to face him and all her anger evaporated when she looked into his eyes. She'd known him so long, and this was the way she remembered him. A cowboy in Wranglers, a white hat, a snap-button Western shirt.

"Don't try to talk me out of this." She grabbed the saddle horn with her left hand. "The one thing I know better than anything else is riding."

"I get that." He reached for the saddle. "At least let me help you."

"You're not going to try to talk me out of it?"

He grinned and winked. She got a little weaker.

"Would it do any good?"

"No, not really." She let him take the saddle. "Where's Caleb?"

"With my mom. She's getting back on her feet." He settled the saddle on the horse's back and reached under him for the girth strap. "She thinks she's going to be up to keeping him after school next week."

"Oh." She bit down on her lip and watched as he slipped the strap through the ring and pulled it tight. "I'm glad she's feeling better."

"Don't tell me you've enjoyed your stint as a baby-sitter."

"I have." She had to let it go. "But he needs stability and I'm the worst person for that."

"You've been great for him." He eased the stirrups into place and adjusted them. "I'll check these for you after you're on him."

Once upon a time she would have flung herself into the saddle, leaned to adjust the stirrups and that would have been the end of it. But Slade made it easy to accept help.

"Is Caleb riding his pony?"

"Not enough kids signed up so they had to scratch pole bending."

"What about the cupcakes? Will he still need them?" She handed Slade the bridle.

"He's counting on you for that party even if he is staying with Mom."

Joy bubbled up and she smiled. "Oh, good. I'm kind of counting on the party, too."

Slade slipped the bridle into place and unhooked the lead.

"Here you go." He stepped back.

She took the reins and grabbed the saddle horn. And then she was in the saddle, settling into the seat, getting her feet adjusted in stirrups that were already close to perfect. She held the reins in her left hand and held the tail of the reins in her right hand, resting her arm on her thigh.

"It's going to be different, Mia. You should take him out in the field and practice a few turns with him."

She nodded and eased the horse around. "Slade, thank you."

He tipped his hat. "Anytime, friend."

Friend. Of course that's what they were. She couldn't let herself believe they were more. She had it figured out now. She had allowed herself to get caught up in all the romance going on around her. Everyone pairing up had made her feel lonely. She could shake that off the way she'd shaken off old sports injuries back in school. It didn't have to hurt.

Pain was an emotion. She could control her emotions.

As she rode away, she looked back at Slade. He had walked to the front of the truck to watch her. She could control her emotions. She repeated it to herself, in case she forgot.

The horse moved under her, helping her to get her mind on something other than Slade. The animal had an easy, fluid gait. She urged him into a canter and when she let the reins touch his neck, she found that he reined like a cutting horse. Travis had a good eye for horses. She had to give him that.

After a few minutes, she turned him back toward the arena. They had an audience. Next to Slade stood Jackson, Travis and her dad. Her stomach clenched a little. She held her chin up to pretend that facing her dad and brothers didn't bother her.

"What in the..." Jackson started, but their dad cut him off with a look.

"You riding tonight?" Tim Cooper asked with an easy smile.

"Thinking I might." She held the reins loose in her

hand and the roan shifted, settling into a calm stance while she talked.

"Nice horse. Is he Travis's?" Tim walked up to the roan and looked him over.

Now she remembered why she never dated. Because of the inquisition. This is how it felt to bring home a boy, or a man, to Cooper Creek. The men of the family lined up, looks of speculation, doubt, on their faces. They sized men up and then grilled them like they were criminals about to go on trial.

"Yes, he's Travis's." She looked at Travis and he shrugged. She mouthed that she was sorry.

"Nice. Travis, is this the horse you brought home from Texas?"

"Yes, sir."

"You got a good deal on him."

Travis shifted, looked at Jackson, looked at Mia and then at their father. He had to be thinking what Mia was thinking, that this was a trick question. "Yes, sir."

"Think he's safe for your sister?"

"Yes, sir. I wouldn't have put her on him if I didn't think she could handle him."

Mia leaned in the saddle. "Listen, I'm a grown woman who has been riding, thanks to you all, since I was eight years old. I think I can make up my own mind about a horse."

Her dad grinned at her. "So do I, chickpea, just making sure. You might be all grown up, but I'm still the dad and I still want you to leave here in one piece tonight."

"I know." She kissed the top of his hat. "I love you."

"I love you, too. Don't beat them too badly."

"I won't."

They all walked away, all but Slade. "Be safe tonight."

"You be safe, too." She smiled what she hoped was a friendly smile.

The announcer spoke. They would play the "Star-Spangled Banner" and then pray. No one ever complained about a prayer at the Dawson Rodeo Arena. People would probably be upset if there wasn't a prayer.

Mia removed her hat and put her hand over her heart as the anthem was sung by a high school girl she knew from church. And then the prayer. She bowed her head and the horse shifted beneath her, settling the weight from one back leg to the other.

Keep us safe. Amen. She looked up at the dark sky. Around her were sights and sounds that were familiar. The wood bleachers, the bright lights, the pens behind the arena where livestock were waiting for events. People spoke in loud voices, some laughed, and music played from several different spots.

She and Butch had always prayed. Briefly she closed her eyes and shook away the moment of pain. A hand touched hers.

"You okay?"

She smiled down at Slade. "I'm good."

He moved his hat back as he stared up at her. "I'm going to get my horse. I'm team-roping with Jackson."

"Go. I'm fine. I really don't need a keeper."

"I know you don't." He looked around and then back up at her and she got it. "Mia, I'm more worried about who is out there."

"Got it. I'm safe." She tightened her fingers around his just briefly. "You be safe, too."

"I always am."

He walked away. She sat easy on the horse and watched him go.

* * *

Slade watched from astride his big gray gelding as Mia rode her horse to the gate. The horse and rider in the arena rounded the first barrel, the second and then hit the third, knocking it over. The horse shimmied to the left and the rider held tight but lost time as she urged the horse forward and down the homestretch back to the gate at the end of the arena.

Mia held the reins of her horse in her left hand and he worried about that. It would throw off everything. Nothing would be the way it had always been when she'd ridden before. The other riders were watching because they all knew who Mia was and what she'd accomplished in this sport. They were nervous for themselves. He was nervous for her.

She needed this sport.

Mia urged the horse forward. Travis said the horse had been used by a college girl who'd barrel-raced for a year before she got bored with it. Mia backed her horse up. The animal knew the game. He started to prance, almost running in place. The gate flew open and the horse flew toward the first barrel. Mia leaned, holding him steady, easy around the barrel. Across to the second barrel. And then to the third. She brought him around the barrel and for a second she looked off balance. The horse stumbled. Mia held him steady and he pushed on, running fast to the gate with Mia leaning low over his neck, her hair flying out behind her. Her hat flew off as she crossed the finish line.

Slade grinned as he watched her bring the horse under control and turn back to get her hat from the kid who had run out to retrieve it. She thanked the boy, wiped dirt off the hat and settled it back on her head.

When she turned toward him he saluted and she

smiled that big Mia smile that lit up her face. He knew, even from a distance, that the sparkle would be back in her eyes. He hoped it would be back for good.

He turned his horse and rode away from the arena. Jackson rode up to him. "Did you see that sister of mine?"

"I did."

Jackson cocked his head to one side and his smile disappeared. "What's going on with the two of you?"

"Nothing, why?"

"Nothing, why?" Jackson mocked. "Because something is eating you, friend."

"Nothing is eating me, Jackson." Slade backed his horse away from Jackson.

"Sure, okay, let's go with that. She's a good person. The two of you have known each other for years."

Slade pulled off his hat. It was a warm night for September. The breeze felt good. "Jackson, I'm pretty aware of how long I've known your sister. I am even more aware that she's a good person."

"Have you noticed lately how stinking pretty she looks on a horse?"

Slade glanced her way.

Jackson laughed and slapped his chaps-covered leg. "Yep, I guess you have. Well, I'd welcome you to the family, but I reserve that right for our grandmother. She's the matchmaker."

"I'm not a member of the family, Jackson. I do not foresee myself changing my name to Cooper."

"Slade Cooper. It does have a ring to it. If I was a guessing man, I'd say a ruby ring with diamonds."

"The woman I marry will take *my* name and I'll buy my *own* ring."

"You do know my grandmother, right?" Jackson

laughed again and to Slade he was starting to sound like a braying donkey.

"Yes, I do know your grandmother." He also knew she had a mighty powerful prayer life. Slade adjusted the coiled rope on his saddle horn. "Think we'd better head that way?"

"I think we probably should. Hey, Slade, I know this is hard for you. I just want you to know…"

Slade held up his hand to stop his friend. "Jackson, I'm not ready."

"I know." Jackson eased the reins back to hold his own horse steady. "Is that horse ready for this?"

"I hope so. He's a little spooked, but I've been roping off him for a month."

Their team was called. Slade eased his horse forward. He glanced at Jackson, who nodded and then leaned forward. They'd done this a hundred times, maybe more. Slade felt his horse move, prepare.

And then the calf was in the arena and their horses leapt forward. Slade held his rope easy in his hand. He glanced toward Jackson but something caught his eye, something to his right. His horse saw it, too. Before he could prepare, Slade's horse went straight up and then jolted to the right. He held tight for about ten seconds, and then he was on the ground looking up at the sky.

He hadn't been thrown like that in years. He moved gingerly, testing his limbs. About the only thing that hurt was his back and his head. He groaned and leaned back. Maybe his horse wasn't quite ready.

Jackson appeared next to him, leaning over and grinning that cheesy grin of his. "You okay?"

"Great. My pride hurts. My back hurts. My head hurts. What happened?"

"Some kid decided to fly a paper airplane into the arena."

"Seriously?"

"For real." Jackson held out a hand. "Anything broken? Can you get up?"

"Yeah, I can get up. But could you tell someone to stop spinning the globe?"

"Hit your head, did you?"

"Yeah. I think I might have blacked out for a second."

"Well, at least you know where you are."

Slade heard a commotion as he reached for Jackson's hand and stood. Everyone clapped and he waved his hat. Yeah, this was humiliating. Nothing like getting thrown off a perfectly good horse in front of everyone you know. The commotion continued. He turned and saw that it was at the gate. The commotion had a name—Mia.

"If you can walk, I'll get our horses." Jackson had his horse by the reins, but Slade's gelding stood close to the fence. "And you can deal with Mia."

"Thanks." He limped toward the exit. The crowds had gone back to their popcorn and talking to the people around them. Rodeo was as much about visiting with neighbors as watching the events, he guessed.

"Are you okay?" Mia opened the gate for him.

"I think so." He rubbed the back of his head and felt a knot the size of a golf ball. "Other than the lump on the back of my head."

"The paramedics are waiting." She took his arm and was practically dragging him toward the ambulance.

"I have a horse I need to tend to and I don't need a paramedic."

"Jackson has your horse. He'll take care of him. Look, it's my turn."

"Your turn?"

"To take care of you."

"Oh." He let her lead him because he didn't feel like arguing. One of the attendants nodded as he headed their way.

"Slade, I didn't expect you over here," the guy said.

"Paper airplane meets horse," Mia explained.

Slade flinched when the guy flashed a light in front of his face. "Could you warn me before you do that?"

"Sorry." Pete was someone Slade saw on a weekly basis. They were often at the same incidents. "If I tell you to go in for a CT, will you?"

"No. If anything, it's a mild concussion." Slade stretched. "And a bruised back."

"You might want to keep an eye on him for a few hours." Pete said this to Mia, who nodded. "He needs to stay awake."

Slade yanked the flashlight out of Pete's hand when Pete started to raise it toward his face a second time. "If you want this back you'll stop flashing it in my face."

Pete laughed and held out his hand. "At least he's conscious and alert. If he does get groggy or his speech gets slurred, headaches…"

"I know, I'll get him to the E.R." Mia looked at him, like she was looking for signs that he might go into a coma.

"I'm fine. I need to check on Caleb."

"I was sitting with him when you went down."

"Nice way to put it. I think the story will be a little more dramatic than the actual event."

"Anyway, he's good. My mom is up there with Heather, Sophie, the whole crew."

"Good to know." He walked away from the ambulance and Mia walked with him.

He thought about telling her she didn't have to baby-sit him, but her hand brushed his, and being alone was suddenly the last thing he wanted.

Chapter Eleven

Mia walked next to Slade, even though common sense told her to walk anywhere but next to him. He walked a little slower than normal. She moved to his right side and slipped her left arm around his waist. He circled his arm around her shoulder. After they'd walked out of the bright circle of lights from the arena he stopped and leaned forward, taking in a deep breath with her hand on his back.

"You're not okay."

"I'm fine." He straightened and turned to face her. "I'm going to be sore tomorrow and the world is a little less than clear right now, but I'm good."

She smiled and reached to wipe dirt off the side of his face. Her hand stilled, her heart and lungs did the same. Complete silence hung between them, and something else, something tangible, strong, pulled them close.

Slade groaned and closed his eyes. "Mia."

"I know."

"I can't think straight."

"Neither can I, and I don't have a concussion."

"I only know that if I don't kiss you right now, I'm not going to get through this night."

"I feel the same way. Then I feel like kissing you is the worst thing I could ever do."

He leaned in close, the brim of his hat touching her forehead. They stood there for a long time, just holding each other, waiting for the moment to pass.

"Remember when we were kids and this was it for us? Every Friday night we were all down here, thinking we'd be young forever, thinking we'd never hurt or cry or want to scream at God."

"I remember." She settled her hands on his waist. His hands were on her shoulders. They kept space between them. Distance.

Mia looked up and he was watching her. They were in the shadows of the trees on a starry autumn night. Slade moved, leaning closer, capturing her mouth with his. They weren't kids anymore. They'd both seen that life could hurt. They'd both found faith again.

Mia let herself be captured by him in that moment. She parted her lips to meet his, needing him the way she had never needed anyone before. She closed her eyes as he swept her away. The world faded, the sounds of the rodeo faded. She let her heart be touched by his. His hands, strong and wide, traveled from her shoulders to her back, holding her close.

"Mia." He withdrew long enough to whisper her name and then he kissed her again.

Mia reached for his hat, took it off and held it at her side. The moment ended, his lips grazed her cheek and settled close to her ear. Mia brushed her lips across the rough plane of his cheeks, feeling the shadow of whiskers from a long day.

"What you do to me…" He shook his head. "I don't know."

"I don't, either."

He cupped her cheeks and kissed her again, just a taste, a sweet taste of what they could be together. "I need time."

"We both need time."

"There's a lot between us."

"Yes."

Her heart wanted to sing. It wanted to cry. Everything she'd never known she wanted was standing in front of her, promising everything—and nothing.

"Mia, I have to think. I have to have space."

"Of course." She moved her hand along his cheek and he grazed her palm with another kiss.

"We should go back."

He took her hand and led her away from that place, that moment, and back to the light of the arena. Back to reality, to the people who would ask questions, speculate.

Caleb saw them first. He was standing with Heather and Elizabeth, and he led them toward Slade and Mia. Heather's expression asked questions. Elizabeth hadn't been a member of the family long enough to give those looks.

Slade let go of her hand and she knew it was because of Caleb. The little boy ran toward them. He looked at Mia and then at his dad.

"You got thrown. You never get bucked off, Dad."

"I know, kiddo. Sometimes it happens, though."

"Are you hurt bad?"

"No, not bad. I'll be sore tomorrow and I have a headache tonight."

"Did Mia make you go to the doctor?" Caleb looked at her. His lips were drawn tight and he narrowed his eyes. Mia didn't know what to say to him.

"No, buddy, she just made me go over and have the

ambulance guys check me out." Slade reached for his son and Caleb jumped into his arms. "I'm fine, Cay."

"Okay, but what if you're not?" For the first time, Mia saw the little boy tear up.

"Of course I'm fine."

Caleb looked at her again. "Is he fine?"

"He's very fine."

Heather snorted and the usually composed Elizabeth actually laughed. Mia glanced at Slade and saw a twinkle in his dark eyes. "Fine?" He mouthed the word.

Heat climbed into her cheeks, a condition she had rarely experienced in her life. She didn't get embarrassed or flustered. She knew how to handle things.

She didn't know how to handle Slade.

"We should get the horses loaded." Mia stumbled over the words and ignored her sister and sister-in-law.

"Of course we should." Slade winced as he shifted Caleb in his arms. "Buddy, I think you're going to have to walk. Your old dad isn't as young as he used to be."

Caleb slid to the ground.

"Thank you for watching him." Slade included Heather and Elizabeth in a smile. "I guess we're going to put up the horses."

Caleb shouted happily and slid between Slade and Mia as they walked away. He held each of their hands, and every now and then holding his legs up in the air to swing between them. Mia watched Slade grimace but he didn't say anything to stop his son.

Travis already had Mia's horse in the trailer. Slade's horse was unsaddled and tied to the back of his trailer. Mia held both of Caleb's hands as his dad put the gelding up. She smiled at Travis when he walked their way.

"Got it all taken care of?" He poked at Caleb's belly and Caleb laughed.

"Yes, I think so. Thanks for taking care of things," Mia answered.

"I could see Slade needed a minute." Travis shrugged it off but his expression turned serious. "What about you? You okay?"

She nodded, but she couldn't really say that she was okay.

Caleb reached for Travis's hand. "Did you see my dad get bucked off?"

"I sure did." Travis took off his hat and set it on Caleb's head. "Did you see me run from that bull that bucked off my brother Gage?"

"I sure did," Caleb imitated with a serious voice. "Where is Gage? My dad says he'll go pro if he keeps his head on."

Mia and Travis both laughed at that. Travis pointed toward the big stock trailer from Cooper Creek Ranch. "He's right over there. But he's cranky and hard to be around."

Mia wondered about that. What had happened to her fun-loving little brothers? Both Gage and Dylan had gone through something, but no one could quite figure out what. Gage was mad at God and everyone else. Dylan had left for Texas six months ago and hadn't been back.

Caleb yawned big. Mia smiled down at him. "Do you want to get in your dad's truck? It's getting kind of cold out here and I'll bet it's warm in there."

Caleb nodded and she noticed that he had sleepy-little-boy eyes. She picked him up with her left arm, holding him close, and carried him to the truck. She got the door open and he crawled in. She found a small pillow and blanket in the backseat of the extended cab.

"Do you want these?"

He nodded and slipped off his dusty cowboy boots, letting them drop on the floor of the truck. Mia put the pillow on the seat and he curled up and grabbed the blanket from her.

"I'm good now. I think I'll just sleep. Can you tell my dad?"

"I'll tell him." She stood there for a minute, wishing she could kiss his cheek and tuck him in. She remembered once that she'd tucked in her brother Lucky's kids when she babysat them for a night.

But that moment didn't compare to this one. She wanted to hug Caleb and hold on to him. She wanted to read him a story and say bedtime prayers with him.

The thoughts rushed at her with the force of a locomotive. She drew in a breath and blinked back the sting of tears. "Good night, Cay."

He gave her a sleepy smile and sat up. Before she could react, his arms were around her neck and he hugged her tight.

"Good night, Mia. No one ever calls me Cay but my dad."

"Oh, I'm sorry."

He was still hugging her tight and he smelled like rodeo, like hamburgers and candy bars and a dusty night. "You can call me Cay."

"Thank you." She kissed his cheek and he let go and settled back in the seat.

It hurt to breathe. She closed the door and wondered how she would get out of this. She had always been good at thinking fast and finding a way out. This time, though, she didn't know if there wasn't an exit or if she just didn't want one.

* * *

Slade stood at the side of the truck, out of the line of sight. He heard his son tell Mia that she could call him Cay. He had watched them hug and watched her tuck his boy in, the way a mom did. The way Slade never managed to. He tried to be both Mom and Dad to Caleb, but the mom gene wasn't in him.

His heart ached worse than his head.

When Mia turned and saw him, she closed her eyes and shook her head. He reached for her hand. At first she didn't take it. Finally, she did and they walked back to the trailer. They leaned against the cold metal, feeling the thing move and shift with the movement of the horse.

"I didn't know." Mia sniffled and he wanted to offer her a handkerchief or tissue. Unfortunately, he wasn't that chivalrous. He guessed his sleeve would do. He held it up and she laughed. "I can't remember ever having a hug like that or feeling that way."

"That's the way it is with a kid." Slade sighed and her fingers tightened on his. "I remember before Vicki had him, I didn't know what I'd do with a kid, how I'd be a dad. And then they put him in my arms and the whole world changed. He's everything, Mia. I can't take one step in this life without thinking about how it will affect him."

"I know."

He rubbed the back of his head. "Man, this hurts."

"Are you sure you don't need to go in and get checked?"

"I'm good."

"He said to keep an eye on you and keep you awake for a few hours."

"I heard him."

They moved to the tailgate of his truck and watched as other trailers were loaded. The bulls in the pens were restless, moving and stirring up dust. Slade heard Jackson yell at Reese to open a gate. Slade watched for his friend. Reese seemed to be doing well. He'd adjusted to his lost eyesight. He'd gotten married and he and his wife had a little boy. But Slade still felt the need to protect the guy who would give his life for anyone.

Cars were pulling out of the parking areas. Slade watched his mom's car go by with Eve in the driver's seat. He waved. They didn't see him.

Next to him Mia moved. He glanced down as she cradled her right arm with her left. She didn't say anything.

He put his arm around her shoulder and drew her close.

"Slade?"

"Um-hmm."

"I don't know what to do. I'm not sure what we're doing."

"I know."

He looked down at their hands, fingers laced together. He clasped and unclasped his fingers over hers.

"I'll be right back." He hopped down off the back of the tailgate and then regretted the sudden jolting movement. He ran his hand along his lower back and groaned. Mia snickered and he turned to look at her.

"You said it—we're not as young as we used to be."

He grinned and almost quoted the words to a Toby Keith song. He didn't. Instead, he dug around in the back of the trailer for an old quilt. Mia watched as he brought it back and spread it out in the back of the truck.

The lights of the arena flickered off. The truck pulling the Cooper Creek trailer idled and then eased out of the parking lot. Travis honked, waved and went on, leaving them alone.

"You said you'd keep an eye on me." He walked to the cab of his truck and peeked in. Caleb was sound asleep, his thumb in his mouth and a happy smile on his face.

Once upon a time, he didn't know how they would ever be happy, just the two of them. But they were. He walked back to Mia and she was straightening the quilt in the back of the truck.

"What's your plan, Slade McKennon?"

"Well, we have a five-year-old chaperone and I'm a gentleman, so my plan just includes the two of us pretending for a little while longer that we're still kids without a care in the world."

"How long do you think we can get away with that?" She moved as he climbed into the back of the truck.

He took her with him, to the quilt. He sprawled out, groaning at the stiff muscles in his back that didn't want to release and let him stretch.

"I give a good back rub. Sit up."

He sat with his back to her. She rubbed the tight muscles and he leaned forward, wishing he could sleep as his body relaxed. Eventually, she stopped and then she kissed his shoulder.

"I'm a gentleman." He relaxed on the quilt again.

"I'm glad." She stretched out, too, but kept space between them. "I'm..."

"What?"

"Waiting."

"For?" He turned to look at her, wondering if she was waiting for him to say something or do something.

"Waiting." She looked away, sighing. "For marriage."

"Oh, wow. Mia." He had never been in love with

Mia. As kids he'd thought she was cute, but she'd been the little sister of his best friend. And then she'd been Vicki's best friend.

Tonight she was one of the most amazing women he'd ever met. Maybe she'd been that person for a while. He slid his hand down her arm and found her hand. The two of them stared up at the stars.

"Aren't you going to laugh, at least a little?" she asked. He shook his head. "I mean, really, did you expect me to tell you that?"

"No, I didn't. But…"

"But you think I'm amazing and not emotionally stunted. Not a workaholic with no life, or something?"

"Amazing." He lifted her hand to his lips and held it there.

But what did he do with the amazing woman next to him? That remained the question of the night, or the question of the year.

"You realize Travis was my ride home." She broke the silence with a change of topic.

He was okay with the change. "Yes, I think I did know that."

"You know I can walk from here. It's not a half mile."

"Right, that's what I'm going to let you do at midnight."

"I've been worse places at midnight."

"I'm sure you have."

"I've been with people who would make my mother blush."

"Do you want to go back to that?"

"Sometimes. There are still people who need to be taken off the street. That job has been my life. I'm not sure how to walk away."

He didn't know what to say. He couldn't argue. He

wouldn't want to walk away from his job. Her job required more. It required her to give up herself for weeks and months at a time.

"Let's not get serious right now," she whispered in the quiet of the night. "We're being young and carefree."

"I know."

"You're getting serious on me. You're thinking about what I do and what it means to my life."

"I guess I am." He was thinking about what it meant to his life in regard to what he felt at that moment. He was thinking about what it meant to Caleb, who talked about her nonstop.

"We are who we are."

"I know that, too."

"You got bucked off tonight." She laughed. "Because of a kid with an amazing paper airplane."

"Thanks for the reminder. I think my back is broken."

"Poor you."

"Yeah, poor me."

She looked at him and then back at the starry sky. "Did you see the shooting star?"

"I missed it."

"Watch more carefully." She giggled a little.

And for a minute they were kids again. Kids in the back of a truck after the rodeo ended. Sore. Happy. Confused. And wanting things they didn't understand. If he thought back a little, this might have been how it felt to be young and falling in love.

Chapter Twelve

After church let out on Sunday, Mia escaped the crowds and walked down the hall to the fellowship room to sign Caleb out of children's church. His grandmother had brought him to church that morning but she had a meeting afterward and asked Mia if she would mind if Caleb stayed with her until Slade got off work. Of course Mia didn't mind. When she saw him peek his blond head around the door, she waved. Madeline, Jackson's wife, pulled him back inside.

"Hey." Madeline smiled and waved. "He said you were going to sign him out. Are the two of you coming to the house for lunch?"

Caleb shook his head and Mia agreed. "No, we have a project we're working on."

"Is the project avoiding your family?" Jackson walked up behind her. "Afraid of the inquisition?"

"You know it, big brother. This show is called the private life of Mia Cooper."

"Let's change it to the 'not so private life.' What do you think of that, sister who stayed behind at the rodeo grounds Friday?"

She glanced down at Caleb. "Little pitchers have big ears."

Caleb looked up at them, squinting and frowning at the saying he'd probably heard more than once.

"Right." He ruffled Caleb's blond hair and the boy glared at him. "Sorry, didn't mean to mess it up."

"Jackson, let it go." Madeline's soft voice of reason. They heard a faint cry from the nursery, and she turned. "That's your son calling you."

"Right, Mama Bear." He kissed her cheek and headed for the nursery. "Lunch, Mia."

"Not today. Next Sunday. I promise."

"I'll hunt you down and drag you to the house if you don't keep that promise." He returned with his baby boy.

"Got it. Now, let me sign this paper, and Caleb and I are history."

As she signed, Caleb hurried to grab his jacket and backpack. "I'm ready."

"Let's go." She looked back toward the sanctuary and opted for the back door.

Caleb hurried next to her, taking big steps for his little legs. "We're gonna make cupcakes?"

She nodded. "Yep, practice run so we know what we're doing for the party."

An hour later they were standing over a bowl, looking at the mess in the kitchen. Caleb had accidentally pulled the beaters up while they'd been on high. Batter flew and chocolate specks dotted the cabinets.

"Cool." Caleb looked around at the mess.

"Yeah, not so cool because you have to help clean this up. But first we put the batter in the cupcake tin. You might have to help because I'm not sure I can do this left-handed."

He nodded solemnly. "Got it."

She put the tin on the counter and handed him the liners to place in each hole. "Make sure you just put one in each."

He went to work putting the pastel-colored liners in place. Mia found a measuring scoop that looked like it would make filling the cupcake liners easy. She hoped. She tried with her right hand, but it was still weak and uncoordinated.

Her left hand wasn't much better. She got a few filled and handed the scoop to Caleb. "Fill it up partway and pour the batter in."

"Got it." Tongue in the corner of his mouth, eyes scrunched, he concentrated and filled the cupcake tin with batter, getting a cupcake's worth on the top of the baking tin.

Mia handed him a paper towel. "Wipe that off or we'll have a real mess."

"Don't you know how to cook?" He wiped, but mostly smeared the batter. She helped with a clean towel.

"A little. I've never really had time." Or anyone to cook for.

"Aren't girls supposed to cook?"

She laughed at that. "Well, I guess we are. But sometimes guys can cook. Like you're doing right now."

"I think it's woman's work."

She hugged him tight. "Oh, little man, we have got to talk more."

He watched from the stool as she put the cupcakes in the preheated oven.

"Now what?" His legs dangled and his boots were loose on his feet.

"Clean the mess. I'll move your stool over to the

sink and you can wash the dishes. I'll wipe down the cabinets."

"Wash dishes!" he said in outrage at what he probably thought was more woman's work.

"You bet." She scooted his stool across the tile floor and he held on tight, laughing and then laughing more because the sound vibrated as the stool scooted.

"What do we do after silly old dishes?" He got up on his knees and swished the bowl in the soapy water.

"We should probably go check on the mare."

"Oh, yeah." He scrubbed the bowl and then moved it to the other side of the sink, spraying it with warm water to rinse it. "Do you think she's broke?"

"I think she probably is."

"How long do cupcakes bake?"

She looked at the recipe. "It says eighteen minutes but that seems like a long time."

"We don't want them burned."

"No, we don't." Mia set the timer on the stove for fourteen minutes. She cleaned the cabinets easily, and the dishes were done quickly, too.

"What time does my dad get here?"

Mia looked at the clock on the wall. "He went in at six this morning, right?"

"I think. I was sleeping at Grammy's house."

"Gotcha. Well, if he went in at six, he should be off by three this afternoon. I think."

"Can we go put a saddle on the horse?" He slid off the stool and Mia shook her head.

"No, not with just the two of us here." She looked in the door of the oven. "We have to take the cupcakes out in a minute. And then we put in the next batch."

Mia's phone rang. She picked it up and answered. "Tina, what's up?"

"Hi, Mia. I was wondering when you'd be in Tulsa again."

"My next appointment is in two weeks. Why?" Mia waited for a response but none came. "Tina, what's going on?"

"I'm a grown woman. I shouldn't be, but I'm afraid. I don't want to have this baby alone. I don't want to be alone."

"Has something happened?"

Mia heard moving, shuffling and Tina talking to her two little ones. "Mia, I think someone was in my house."

"When?"

"While I was at church. I know I locked the door. I mean, maybe I didn't. It could be that I forgot, but I'm sure I didn't."

"Was anything taken or messed with?"

"Not that I can tell."

"I want you to come here. There's an apartment at my parents' place. There's a hospital in Grove. We'll work it out."

"I don't know."

"You can't stay there, Tina. Put the kids in the car. Don't worry about packing too much. We can get what you need when you get here. Just get in the car and start driving."

Tina sobbed on the other end of the line. "Mia, I don't know, maybe it's nothing. Maybe I'm just lonely and the baby is due soon."

"Tina, I need to have you here so I can keep you safe. And if you're here, you won't be lonely."

"I don't want you to think you're my responsibility."

"I made a promise." She closed her eyes, trying hard

to block memories of Butch and of her telling him she would look out for Tina and the kids.

"I would like to come there." Tina cried and the two of them stayed on the phone until her tears stopped.

"Leave now. Don't look obvious. Just shove what you can in maybe the kids' backpack, or even a laundry basket. Call 911 if you feel threatened in any way. I'll be waiting for you to call when you get close to Dawson. And call me when you're on the road so that I know you're safe."

"Okay, I'll leave in fifteen minutes." The call ended.

Suddenly the smoke detector was going off and smoke filled the air. Caleb ran through the kitchen, yelling that they needed the fire department. "Quick!"

Mia grabbed a broom and knocked the smoke detector off the wall before she opened the oven door. Smoke rolled out. "Calm down. It isn't a fire."

She turned off the stove and found an oven mitt so she could pull out the blackened cupcakes. The stench of burned chocolate filled the air. Next to her Caleb coughed and covered his mouth and nose. Mia carried the cupcake tin to the sink and dropped it in.

"Well, that proves one thing. I can't bake."

Caleb moved his hand from his mouth and nose. "We can buy cupcakes."

"What in the world is going on in here?"

Mia turned and smiled at her grandmother. "We're baking?"

Granny Myrna looked in the sink. "Land's sakes, that's a mess. I don't think you can call that baking. More like you're burning. Now, what it is it the two of you are up to?"

"Cupcakes for a school party next week," Mia explained as she opened windows and turned on the exhaust fan over the stove.

"Well, why would you be making them this soon?" Her grandmother peeked at the batter and wrinkled her nose.

"This is a test run."

"Good thing." She mixed the batter with a spoon. "Did you put too much oil in this?"

"No." Mia looked at the batter. She hadn't noticed before that it looked oily. She looked at Caleb and he shrugged.

"I think this needs to go down the drain." Granny Myrna carried the bowl to the sink and ran water in it, flipping on the garbage disposal. "What day do we need these cupcakes?"

"Next Thursday."

"Well, when the time comes, the two of you come over and we'll make the cupcakes at my house the night before. No sense poisoning little children."

"Thanks, Gran." Mia hugged her grandmother and then stepped back to give her a look. "What are you doing here?"

"Checking on my granddaughter, of course. Once again you skipped lunch at the ranch and I wanted to make sure you're okay. And I can see that you are."

"I'm good. Slade had to work and Caleb's grammy had a luncheon." She glanced at the clock on the stove. "Slade should be here anytime."

"Well, since you're doing so well, I won't stay." Her grandmother hooked an arm through Mia's. "Walk me to my car."

Mia glanced back at Caleb. "Why don't you turn on the TV and we'll have a snack when I get back in."

Caleb didn't have to be told twice. Obviously, little

boys weren't crazy about baking. But they were crazy about cartoon superheroes.

Mia walked out the front door with her grandmother. They took slow steps, her grandmother leaning a little more on the cane she seldom used.

"Gran, you feeling okay?"

"Of course I am." Myrna stopped walking. "Don't let this cane fool you. I'm not ready for the rocking chair."

"Of course you aren't. I just asked if you're okay."

"I'm good." Her grandmother's smile faded. "I'll tell you the truth, Mia. I'm not as young as I used to be. And neither are you."

"Ouch."

"I guess I'm wondering what the whole family is wondering."

"What's that?" Mia should have gone to the family lunch, if for no other reason than to stop the talk.

"If you're going to stay in Dawson and settle down. And I know that's selfish of us. But we love you and want you here with us. You know how we worry when you're gone."

Mia kissed her grandmother's cheek. "I do know. And Gran, I just can't tell you yet what I'm going to do because I still don't know."

"Well, as long as you pray about it, and know that we're praying for you."

"I'm praying." And she was finding faith. She was even learning who she was without her job. No matter what, she was still Mia.

They continued walking, reaching her grandmother's car just as Slade pulled into the drive. "There's that Slade McKennon. He's a fine-looking man."

"Yes, Gran, he is."

"Well, I'm glad your eyesight is still good. I was

starting to worry if you could see what was right in front of your face."

Mia laughed a little and opened the car door. Myrna hesitated.

"Are you trying to rush me?"

"If I admit I am, will I be in trouble?" Mia glanced in Slade's direction again. He had stepped out of his truck and was settling his hat on his head.

"Oh, I think you're in more trouble than you realize." Myrna patted her cheek and slid behind the wheel of her car. "You behave, Mia. Slade, don't forget I have something I need for you to haul out of my house."

Slade walked up to the car and leaned in. "I haven't forgotten, Mrs. Cooper. I'll try to get by there one day this week."

"Good boy. Now close my door. And don't eat anything this young woman cooks. I swear she'd poison you with that stuff she's been mixing up."

Slade closed the door and Myrna cranked the engine to life. They stepped away as she backed out of the driveway and pulled out onto the road.

"Your grandmother is a case."

Mia smiled as she watched the car drive away. "I don't know what I'd do without her."

"I take it the cupcakes were a success?" Slade asked as they walked up the sidewalk to the house.

"It depends on your definition of *success*. If you mean because I know for sure my smoke alarms work, yes, they were a success."

"Good to know."

They found Caleb sleeping on the couch. Mia smiled at the little guy and she tried not to think about the fact that he would be staying with his grandmother again.

She didn't want to think about not seeing him if she did return to work.

She didn't want to think about not seeing Slade.

"Thanks for watching him today."

"Anytime." She watched as he bent to pick his son up. "How are you feeling?"

Slade hefted Caleb to his shoulder. "Better. Headache is gone. My back is still a little stiff."

"Remember, if you need me to watch him, I'm here."

"I'll remember." He eased through the front door and she held it open for him. "Are you trying to rush me out of here for some reason?"

"Nope. I mean, I have things to do. Like clean up the mess in the kitchen, but other than that…" She shrugged as if that was it, nothing going on.

He gave her a suspicious look. "Mia, is everything okay?"

She kissed his cheek and then Caleb's. "Everything is fine. Take him home. He wants a nap and he mentioned riding that new pony of his."

"Call me…"

"If I need anything. I know."

She watched him leave and then hurried back inside to finish getting ready for Tina. She figured she had another hour, tops, to put clean sheets on the beds, wipe down the bathroom and sweep the kitchen floor.

When she heard a car pull in her drive she hurried out to help Tina. But it wasn't Tina, it was Slade.

Slade had a funny feeling about Mia. He had kind of guessed she was up to something, so on the way to his house, he asked Caleb a few questions. What he got were bits and pieces of a phone conversation his son had overheard. Which was why he had dropped his son off with his mom and headed back to town.

Mia walked out the front door as he drove in. She had changed into shorts and a T-shirt. Her hair was pulled back in a ponytail. And she didn't look at all happy to see him. If she asked why he was there, he didn't know what he'd tell her.

What she did wasn't any of his business. She'd tell him that no matter what excuse he came up with for butting into her business. He should be telling himself exactly the same thing. She was a friend, but he wasn't her keeper.

He got out of the truck, pocketing his keys.

"I didn't expect you back so soon." She looked past him and she looked more than a little worried.

"I know." He walked up the steps. "So why the big hurry to get me out of here earlier?"

"I wasn't in a big hurry."

"Really? That isn't how I saw it." He had to keep his focus. He had to look at the situation and not at her. That wasn't easy to do, and he'd had years of practice when it came to keeping focus.

"Well, I'm sorry if I seemed to be rushing you. I had a big mess to clean up and the mare needed my attention." Her eyes darted to the road again.

"Mia, I don't have time for you to try to bulldoze me. Caleb told me you got a call from Tina."

"Oh."

"Yeah, oh."

"She did call." Her eyes darted away again and then back. She smiled sweetly. "Look, Slade, I really can handle this."

"Handle what?"

"I told Tina to come and stay with me for a while.

I might put her up at the ranch. But she needs to be somewhere safe."

"And what about you? Does it jeopardize your safety if you bring her here?"

"That's compassionate."

He brushed a hand through his hair and sighed. "Mia, I'm compassionate. I'm also aware that she's in trouble and until she tells everything she knows, there's no way to help her."

"Right, I get that. I know she's in trouble. But I also know that I held her husband when he died and I promised I'd take care of Tina and the kids. I can't take care of them if they're in Tulsa."

"There are police officers in Tulsa who can take care of her."

Mia let the screen door close behind her. She stepped down so that she was directly in front of him. She wasn't a tiny little thing who needed to be protected. She was Mia. She could probably take him in a fair fight. And that was hard to swallow.

But for a moment he saw the softness in her eyes, the lack of objectivity. Steely resolve quickly took its place. Her dark eyes sparked with stubborn pride.

"Slade, I'm better than they are."

"Oh, really?"

She shrugged a little. "Yes, really. And I'll be with her all the time, not patrolling once an hour."

"And you'll put yourself in harm's way." He let the words out and ignored that they were the real reason he had a problem with this. He didn't want her hurt.

He had lost his wife because she decided to run an errand for him that he should have done himself. He should have been there and stopped her. The guilt had almost killed him. He'd kept going for Caleb's sake.

"Slade?" Mia touched his arm. "What is it?"

"Nothing." He shook it off and focused on her. "I know I can't talk you out of this."

"No, you can't. She's here." She nodded in the direction of a car coming up the road. "And she's going to stay here until we figure out who is doing this and why."

"Then I'm calling county and state. They need to know what's going on."

"Do what you have to do. But first, help me get them in the house and settled."

"Fine, I'll help you get her settled. At the ranch."

"What?"

"My place, Mia. We'll take her out to the trailer on my mom's place. Gray hasn't been home in months. He's got a girl out in Colorado he's in love with and he's found a job on a ranch there. We might as well have someone living in the place."

"And put your mom in the middle of this?"

"My mom is as handy with a shotgun as you are with your service revolver."

"Yes, but the point of bringing her here is that she's scared. She's been having contractions. She doesn't have family."

"And if she's at the Circle M, she'll have my mom. She'll have me. She'll have you trespassing every chance you get."

"I'm a trespasser now?" She vaguely smiled and he flicked her chin with his finger and thought about kissing her.

"No, you're not trespassing."

Her smile faded and the light in her brown eyes dimmed.

"I think maybe I'm trespassing on very private property. A place I have no right to go."

"Oh, Mia." He shook his head and glanced toward the car with the woman and two kids. "We can't talk about this right now."

"No, you're right. That was wrong. And yes, the trailer is good. No one will think to look for her there."

"Let's go tell her. Lock your doors, because I know you're going out there with us."

"You guessed right. And on my way home, I'm picking up my new dog. Or my new stray."

"You do know how to bring home strays."

"It's who I am, Slade. It's the only way I know how to be."

"I know."

Slade had to let it go. This was Mia. She would always be this person, putting her own safety on the line to protect and serve. It was the way she'd been wired from early on, a result of her childhood. He'd either have to accept it or keep his distance.

Chapter Thirteen

The trailer was an eighties model, decorated in shades of dusty-rose and powder-blue. It also had a collection of crazy posters featuring television beauties, old rodeo stars and rock bands. Mia took one look at the living room and laughed.

Slade stepped in behind her, carrying one of Tina's sleeping children, Jackie. Mia had spent hours discussing Butch's family with him. Even though she hadn't met them until the funeral, she knew them. She knew that Jackie was four and loved to color pictures of princesses. Mia had even bought her a stack of coloring books for Christmas last year. Jason was three and loved fire trucks like every little boy. The louder, the better. Butch had not thanked her for that gift, the one that had the siren and the horn that would make you check your rearview mirror if you had the toy in the car.

"What's so funny?" Slade placed the sleeping child on the hunter-green-and-burgundy-plaid sofa that clashed with the powder-blue carpet.

Mia pointed at the walls. "Hey, Tina, do you love what we've done with the decor?"

For the first time Tina cracked a real smile. Butch

had met her in college. She had a teaching degree but had given up her career when she realized his job would keep them separated so much of the time. She'd told Mia a few weeks ago that she planned to go back to teaching.

"It looks like early-American teen," Tina offered.

"My brother Gray. He's matured slower than most. Go ahead and take them down. I don't think you want the kids to have nightmares."

Tina shook her head, her light brown hair swinging. "No, I don't mind. It's his place and he should come back to it the way it is."

"If he comes back, he'd better be grown up enough that he doesn't want these posters on the walls." Slade growled and Mia gave him a look. Gray was in his mid-twenties now and she hadn't seen him a lot, but he couldn't be that bad.

"I'll take them down," Mia offered. She started removing tacks, tossing them in a cup on the counter. "Tina, we can run into Grove tomorrow and stock up on groceries. And my brother Jesse is a doctor. He can get you an appointment with an OB friend of his."

"Mia, I don't know how to thank you. I already feel better, just being far from Tulsa. Maybe I just needed to get away from the apartment and the memories."

Mia looked at Slade when Tina made that confession. She knew that he would understand. He would get where Tina was coming from. And for a moment she felt jealous. The emotion tasted like bile and she forced it down.

"Mom is going to bring over some leftover meat loaf and mashed potatoes." Slade carried in the laundry basket filled with what looked like dirty clothes.

Mia smiled at Tina, because she had listened to Mia's advice. If anyone saw her leaving her apartment, they would have thought she was going to do a load of laundry. Slade looked at the clothes and at Mia.

"Your idea?" He set the basket down on the tiny kitchen table.

"Of course."

He shook his head and smiled. "Mom also has some lunch meat and bread in the freezer. She freezes everything. She'll be over here soon and you'll probably have enough to last several days."

"I don't know how to thank you." Tina hugged herself tight and for a second her face tightened.

"Contractions?" Slade asked.

"Yes. I've been keeping track. I'm having them every thirty minutes. They should go away when I put my feet up."

Mia pointed to a rocking recliner. "Then put your feet up because we have a lot to do before you can have Junior. I'm going to put clean sheets on the beds and make sure the bathrooms are somewhat clean."

"I can help," Tina offered and started to follow.

Slade stepped forward. "I'll give her a hand."

Mia laughed at that. "Good thing, because mine doesn't really work."

He gave her a look and then followed her down the hall. She found clean sheets in the closet and blankets. The tiny second bedroom had a twin bed and a dresser. The main bedroom had a queen bed that filled up the small room and a private bathroom.

Slade stripped the sheets that were on the bed.

"We're doing the right thing," Mia said as she flipped the sheet his way.

"I know."

"You could stop looking so growly."

He shook his head and finished tucking the corners

of the sheet. "No, I can't. How am I supposed to be calm about your putting yourself in danger?"

"She's in danger, not me." Mia tossed him the pillowcases. "Sorry, I can't do them. I can spread a blanket but pillowcases are still tough."

"How's the physical therapy going? Are you doing your exercises?"

"Of course. Jesse stops by from time to time to check on me and help out." She held her hand out and made something resembling a fist. "See, I can almost do it."

But it hurt and it was weak and sometimes the weakness made her want to cry. The pain she could deal with, the weakness she couldn't. Slade placed the pillowcases on the bed and then he was at her side, his arms were around her waist. She leaned into him, breathing in deep of his scent, holding on to the moment so that it would be a memory later.

"You make me crazy," he whispered, his breath soft on her neck.

"Yeah, well, join the club." She thought about listing the ways he wreaked havoc on her world.

Her phone beeped. She pulled it out and walked away from Slade. Her hands trembled as she pushed the button and retrieved the message.

"Something important?" He had walked up behind her.

"Kind of." She read the message and her insides shook.

"Mia, what's wrong?"

She held up a picture. "Slade, this is my sister Breezy. I've been looking for her and now, maybe I've found her."

"Be careful." His low warning took her by surprise.

"What?"

"There are people on those sites who pose as people…"

"Slade, I know all that. I'll be careful. But I need to find her. She's part of my heart. I've spent years worrying, wondering where she went to."

"You never knew?"

She shook her head. "No. Mom tried to find her for me, but they vanished, she and her grandmother. You know, don't you, that my siblings and I had different fathers? Breezy's grandmother lived out of state, but she drove to Oklahoma and picked her up. We never heard from her again."

"Where is she?"

"Somewhere in California. This is from an agency out there."

"Agency?"

"I found a website and they help bring separated siblings together."

"I see." He looked again at the page she showed him on her phone.

"But you're skeptical, Mr. Detective."

"I'm always skeptical. But I want this for you."

She kissed his cheek. And then someone knocked on the door and his mom yelled, "Yoo-hoo," from the living room.

Saved by the mom. Mia let out a breath and walked down the hall.

Slade smiled at the two little kids who had woken up. Caleb had them engaged in animated conversation about the puppies a stray dog had given birth to under the front porch and then he started telling them about the horses and cows and asking them if they liked animals. The kid barely took a breath before he rushed on to a discussion about school.

Slade's mom, Marty, smiled at her grandson and placed a calming hand on his head. "Take a break, Caleb."

"Mom, this is Tina. Tina, my mom, Marty Mc-Kennon."

"It's so good to meet you, honey." Slade's mom walked to the kitchen with the bags she had carried in. "Now you tell me if there's anything at all you need. I see someone already took down those horrible posters of Gray's."

"Mia did that," Slade explained as he walked up behind his mom and kissed her cheek. "Thanks for bringing things over."

"No problem. Now I can't stay because I have a show I'm not going to miss tonight and my DVR isn't recording. But if Tina needs anything at all, I'm just a shout away. And from the looks of you, honey, you might be needing a ride to the hospital anytime."

Tina's eyes filled with tears as his mom poured sympathy on her. His mom was good at that, and he'd been right to bring Tina here. He could tell from the look on Mia's face that she agreed.

"Thank you, Mrs. McKennon."

"Now, you call me Marty. We're all just family around here." Marty sat down on the edge of the couch and rested a hand on Tina's arm. "Have you been timing the contractions?"

Tina closed her eyes and nodded. "Every thirty minutes. But the last one didn't seem as strong. I think resting helps."

"Do you think she should be here alone?" Marty looked at Mia, not at him.

"I'm not sure." Mia had taken a seat on the end of the old coffee table and Caleb gravitated to her, crawling up on her lap as if he was meant to be there. Slade saw his life getting more complicated by the minute.

"Well, I suppose we're all right here, but I'd feel better if someone stayed the night here with her." His mom sounded like the final vote.

"Slade was going to take me home. He can run me home to get clothes and bring me back."

"That's a good idea." Marty patted Tina's arm and stood. "Honey, you're going to have that baby in the next week. Mark my words."

Tina closed her eyes and nodded.

"Well, my show isn't that important." Marty smiled sweetly. "Slade, take Mia home so she can pack a bag. I'll wait here and I'll warm up something for supper."

Slade had been the master of his own life just a few short weeks ago. Or at least he'd thought that was the way it worked. Now he stood in a two-bedroom trailer very much not in control of a thing, as far as he could tell.

Mia had turned to face him and she looked as if she might start laughing at any minute. "Ready to go?"

"Cay, are you staying here with Gram or going with me?"

"Staying!" He had opened his backpack to reveal toys he must have shoved in before coming over to meet the new kids.

"Mom?" Slade had to ask.

"Of course he can stay."

Slade walked out the door with Mia. His hand went to the small of her back as they walked down the narrow steps of the trailer.

"You should have left her at my house." Mia walked with him to his truck.

"You think you're always right." He opened the door for her and she climbed in. Out of habit he reached for the seatbelt and pulled it across her. She sucked in her breath and waited for him to click it into place.

And then his face was close to hers and she shook her head.

"Let it go, cowboy."

"Making. Me. Crazy."

"That makes two of us."

He pulled onto the main road a few minutes later and reached to turn up the radio. Kenny Chesney sang about his tractor and Mia sang along.

"You're okay with this?" he asked as they turned into Dawson.

"With staying at the trailer tonight?" She shrugged. "I would prefer my house. I know the lay of the land and where my..."

"Weapons are?" He grinned at her.

"A girl does like to be prepared."

"Of course she does. And that's what every girl thinks of when she thinks prepared. Weapons."

"A certain kind of girl does think that way."

He laughed with her and they pulled up in front of her house. "Mia, what are we going to do?"

"Shoot him if he comes close to her?"

"I mean about us."

"I don't know." She didn't make a move to get out. "Do we have to talk about it now?"

"It's the elephant in the room, don't you think?"

She shook her head and reached for the door. "No, it isn't. What's going on with us is not the elephant in the room."

"Then what is?"

She sighed and looked at him. "Vicki. I'm not Vicki. I'll never be Vicki. I'm wild and reckless. I have a career that annoys you. And every time I kiss you, I feel like I'm betraying my best friend."

"You sure know how to fight dirty." He got out of the truck because he didn't know what else to say to her.

Mia rounded the truck and grabbed his hand. "I'm not fighting and this isn't dirty. This is reality. Us. Vicki. My job. It's the way it is and until we figure it out, there's just sweet kisses and heartache."

He cupped her cheeks in his hands and brushed his fingers back into the thick brown hair that smelled of honeysuckle and springtime.

"I don't know what to do, Mia." He rested his forehead against hers.

"Then let's just take a deep breath and back up." She stepped away from him. "I need to pack a bag. Can you feed and water the mare?"

"Yes."

"Slade?"

He stopped and looked back. "What?"

"It's okay, that you still love her. It's understandable. What the two of you shared was special. It was forever. That's not something you get over."

"No, it isn't." He had more to say, but not now. He had loved Vicki. They would have loved each other forever.

Vicki had filled up his whole heart. He didn't know how to open that heart up, or even if there was room in it to love someone else the way he'd loved her. Mia deserved to be loved completely.

The front door closed. He walked around the house and out to the barn. The mare trotted up to the fence but stopped when she saw him. Obviously, the horse had expected Mia. He talked in low tones and she walked up to the fence, dipping her nose in the water trough and then swishing it around and dipping it again.

"No wonder Caleb likes you." He turned on the water and opened the gate to walk out to the barn. "He likes your owner, too."

After all these years of it being just him and Caleb, something had changed since Mia came to town. She was different than having his mom as the third person in their lives. Mia filled a different spot in Caleb's life. She laughed and hugged and played.

It had been safe letting her into their circle. She hadn't been a woman he was dating who would be around temporarily while he tried to enjoy an evening out in adult company, pretending to move on.

Mia had been safe. He laughed at that as he filled a can with grain and dumped it in a rubber feed pan for the mare. Mia could never be considered safe. He should have known better. She was in and out of their lives. She didn't know how to be cautious.

He fed the mare and watched as she slid the grain around the pan. She lifted her head and looked at him with a long stare before going back to her feed.

Before walking away, he patted her neck and she turned to slobber oats on his arm. He brushed his sleeve and walked out the gate. Mia met him outside the back door. She'd changed into sweats and a T-shirt. An overnight bag was sitting on the patio next to her.

"I'm sorry." She picked up the duffel bag and he took it from her. "I pushed. I don't know why. We've always been friends, Slade. I don't want to lose that."

"Neither do I."

"I know that what I said hurt. I don't want to hurt you. I don't want to push you away."

"You aren't hurting me or pushing me away. I guess you're making me think and maybe I wasn't ready to think."

"Let's just let it go."

"I'm not sure if I want to." He surprised himself with the words. "I'm not sure what I want, but I know I've been happier the last few weeks than I've been in a long, long time."

"I don't know if I can deal with the guilt."

"Because Vicki was your friend?" He rested his hand on her arm. "She isn't coming back. I've had to deal with that reality every single day for five years. You've been running from it."

Mia shook her head and tears filled her eyes. "Don't."

"You have to. You have to cry and let her go."

"It isn't that easy."

"I think I know that."

Mia blinked fast and focused somewhere off to his left. "I catch myself sometimes thinking that when I come home she'll be here. Or I want to call her and tell her what's happening in my life."

"I know."

"Being gone made it easier to believe she was still here."

And then she was in his arms. He hugged her tight, fisting his hands in her dark hair as he held her against his shoulder.

Mia sobbed into his neck—huge, racking sobs. Her tears soaked his shirt. Her body heaved as she let go. He held her tight and tried to make sense of how they would go on from here.

"I'm sorry." She finally stopped crying and just held tight to him and he held her back.

"You needed a good cry."

"Says the man who always feels rock-solid."

"I've had my moments."

"I've had more in the last two months than I've had my whole life. I remember crying when I was a kid and then realizing no one paid attention to my tears."

Another peek into her life, her childhood. He thought about God looking down on that little girl and knowing the perfect home, the place where she'd be loved and heard.

He thought about the past five years of his life. He guessed God had been looking down on him, too. He didn't know how to fit Mia into thoughts of God knowing what he needed.

Complicated. The word that fit everything about Mia Cooper. It even described the way he felt about her.

Chapter Fourteen

Mia walked up the sidewalk to the elementary school on Thursday, feeling very much like someone who didn't belong. But she knew how to play a role. She'd been doing it all her life. She'd played the role of mother, taking care of her siblings. She'd played at being a daughter, at being a Cooper, until it finally fit and became who she was. And in her job she had played so many different people she'd lost track.

So today she could wear this skirt and blouse. She could carry the cupcakes she and Caleb had made with Granny Myrna. She could be the class mom. For Caleb, because he needed someone to fill that role.

But she didn't fit. She looked around at the other moms. She knew most of them. She'd gone to school with them. She'd been friends with a few.

They weren't pretending. They were wives and moms. They knew how to bake. They knew how to be social and talk to one another.

Mia walked through the front door of the school and started down the hall. A woman yelled for her to stop. Mia turned, smiling, thinking the woman wanted to say hello. The lady looked anything but happy.

"You have to sign in and get a visitor's pass," the security monitor announced in a loud voice. Everyone turned to stare at Mia with her box of cupcakes.

"Oh, I'm sorry." She should have known that. She smiled at the few women around her.

A woman with curly brown hair came to her rescue. "Mia Cooper?"

"Um, yes?" Mia studied the pixie face with green eyes hidden behind thick glasses. "Cindy?"

"Yes, now Cindy Holder. Remember me, from Ag class?"

"Yes, of course." Mia glanced at the angry office worker who still waited, clipboard in hand. Hopefully she didn't have a Taser. "I have to sign in."

"Of course." Cindy walked her over to the office. "Who are the cupcakes for?"

"Caleb McKennon. He's in kindergarten."

"Oh, of course. I can take them down," Cindy offered with a good-natured smile.

"Um, actually, no." Mia held tight in case someone did try to take them from her. She'd worked hard on those cupcakes. She and Caleb had thrown frosting at each other and eaten the cupcakes that didn't pass the test. "I told Caleb I'd bring them and stay for the party."

"Oh, room mom?" Cindy turned a little pink. "I mean…"

"It's okay. He just wanted me to come to the party."

"Of course." Cindy placed an easy hand on her arm. "I'm so glad you're in town. How long are you staying?"

Mia signed her name on the clipboard and got her visitor's pass. She smiled at the hall monitor who was just doing her job to keep kids safe.

"Do you know where the kindergarten class is?"

"This way." Cindy started down the hall and Mia

caught up. "I'm actually going that way myself. My little girl is in kindergarten. And she just loves Caleb."

"I'll bet she does. He's going to be a cutie when he grows up."

They reached the classroom with fall leaves decorating the doorway. Cindy motioned Mia through the door. She could do this. She could be the "mom" for an hour. For Caleb. She could smile at the other moms and pretend she watched daytime television. She could pretend she knew all about slow-cooker recipes and freezer meals.

She smiled, wondering how they would feel if she talked about her average day. DNA samples, synthetic marijuana, bath salts that didn't go in a tub of water and knowing if an apartment was wired with explosives.

Out of her depth. Yes, cupcakes, homerooms and construction-paper fall leaves—definitely unfamiliar territory.

She put the cupcakes decorated in autumn orange, brown and red on the table with the other treats. Cindy said something about people they went to school with and Mia should come talk to them. She nodded but she stood frozen in the center of the room.

Maybe she wasn't as good at playing a role as she thought.

"Mia!" Caleb ran across the room and jumped at her. She picked him up, holding him in her left arm, her right hand on his arm.

"Hey, buddy, I brought our cupcakes."

"They're going to be the best." He slipped to the ground and told her he had to get back in line for a game. She watched him go, smiling at his energy and exuberance.

He was all Vicki. He had her smile, her joy and her energy. But he had Slade's love of adventure.

Mia waited on the sidelines, watching as the other moms started placing treats on the table and filling cups with an orange drink. As a Cooper she knew this role. She offered to help. The moms looked at her funny, because they knew she didn't belong.

Cindy came to her rescue. "Do you want to put out the paper plates, one on each desk? And a napkin to go with each plate."

"Thank you. Yes."

She took the stack of plates and napkins and started around the room. The other women watched, sometimes sneaking a word or two when they thought she wasn't watching. She kept smiling because this was for Caleb.

From the corner where he stood with the other children, Caleb grinned at her as he blew bubbles through a large hoop. The little boy next to him asked if Mia was his mom. He grinned and nodded. Mia nearly corrected him, because she didn't want him to lie. She didn't want him to need her that much.

She would never fill Vicki's shoes. She would never be the person who felt comfortable in this room with these women, passing out cupcakes and talking about the latest episode of their favorite afternoon talk show.

She had shot a man. She'd held her partner while he died. She definitely wasn't anyone's mom.

If she had any sense at all, she would leave. She should make an excuse and tell Caleb she had to go take care of something, anything that would get her out of here.

Behind her Caleb shouted in victory. She turned and watched him jump through the hoop. He shouldn't have. She knew it the minute she saw him take the leap.

He fell face-first on the tile floor. For a second everything stood still. He didn't cry. No one moved. And then
he stood and turned around and the kids all screamed.

Mia hurried forward. "Caleb, buddy, hold still."

Someone pushed napkins into her hand. She held
them to his nose and his eyes started to water. She
leaned in close and told him it had to hurt and it was
okay to cry. But he didn't cry. He shook his head no
and blinked fast.

Cry. She wanted to tell him to cry, to let it out and not
hold it in. But there were kids and parents surrounding
them. She shifted him into her shoulder and he wrapped
his arms around her and buried his face.

"It's okay to cry," she whispered again. "Sometimes
I cry."

He nodded into her shoulder.

"Should we take him down to the nurse?" Cindy
pulled a chair up and placed it behind Mia. "Here, have
a seat. It's child-sized, but better than squatting on the
floor."

"Thanks. And I think he's going to be fine." She
kept the pressure on his nose and told him to breathe
through his mouth if he could.

Another mom brought an ice pack. She placed it
on his nose and touched Mia's shoulder. "You're doing
great."

No, she was just playing a role. Caleb didn't belong
to her. She held on to him and she wanted to cry, too.

Slade walked through the door of the classroom into
crazy kid drama. Little girls started to shout and they
were all telling him a story, all at once, making it im-
possible to understand. Across the room he saw Mia's
dark head and Caleb's blond head against her shoulder.

"He fell," Cindy Holder explained as he crossed the room to his son and Mia. "He won the bubble-blowing contest and before we could stop him he decided to show everyone he could go through the hoop like the bubbles."

"And he couldn't." Slade smiled at the spirit of his son. Caleb would always believe he could.

"Exactly. Face-first on the floor." Cindy laughed just a little. "But Mia handled it."

He nodded and his gaze landed on Mia cradling his son, handling things. She was holding his little boy, whispering comforting things in his ear and cleaning his face. Slade had a whole mess of tangled-up feelings that he didn't want to deal with at the moment.

He squatted next to the chair Mia sat in and put his hand on Caleb's back. He guessed he was hoping that Caleb would climb into his lap. Instead, his son turned to look at him, but he stayed planted on Mia's lap. Slade didn't much blame him, but it hurt a little. He was used to Caleb turning to him for comfort.

"How are you, Cay?" He put a finger under his son's bruised chin and examined his swollen nose. "You're going to have a shiner."

"What's a shiner?" Caleb asked on a sob.

"Black eyes, because I think your nose is broken."

Caleb's eyes got big and teared up. "Can you fix it?"

"I can't, but a doctor can. Looks like we need a trip to the emergency room. Your first, but probably not your last."

"I should have stopped him." Mia looked about ready to cry, too.

"Mia, things happen. Kids get hurt."

"Not on my watch." She held Caleb a little tighter and his son groaned.

"Maybe don't squeeze the air out of him."

She loosened her hold. "Oh, I'm sorry, Cay. I'm really sorry. I'm not good at this…"

She looked at Slade and he thought he knew what she'd been about to say. She wasn't good at being a mom. But she looked like a natural to him. It just wasn't a role she had planned on filling.

"Party's over, Cay. Time to go see if Dr. Jesse is at the clinic."

"Is Mia going?" Caleb held tight to her neck and Slade looked at her, letting her give the answer.

"Of course I'll go." She stood with Slade's son still in her arms.

"Does this mean I don't get a cupcake?" Caleb held his arms out to Slade and Slade had to admit, it eased his heart a little that his kid still wanted him.

"I'll get you a cupcake." Mia started to walk away from them but Cindy Holder had heard and was already packing up treats for Caleb.

The other moms watched with interest and then the teacher regained control of the situation and found jobs for everyone, jobs that didn't include putting Slade and his son in the middle of whatever drama they were all cooking up in their minds.

He started for the door and Mia caught up with them.

Fifteen minutes later they were sitting in the emergency room waiting for Jesse Cooper to finish with a patient who had more serious injuries. They had tried the clinic in Dawson but Jesse had been called to the hospital, leaving just a receptionist at the clinic that sat next to the Dawson Community Center.

"Mr. and Mrs. McKennon with Caleb." The woman standing in the doorway that led to the emergency room looked at her clipboard and then glanced around the room, smiling at them.

"Mr. McKennon," Mia corrected quickly and as Slade stood, she didn't make a move to join him.

He grinned at her, winking and loving that her cheeks turned pink beneath her tanned skin. "Come on, *Mrs. McKennon,* I think Caleb wants you back there with him."

Caleb nodded over his shoulder and Slade waited, watching Mia and wondering what crazy emotions he saw flickering in her dark brown eyes. If he had to guess, he'd probably go with the one that came to him first. She was thinking about running. This was getting too close, too involved.

"Mia."

She stood and followed them back to the cubicle the nurse led them to. A few minutes later Dr. Jesse Cooper walked through the curtain, pushing it aside as he looked at the chart in his hands. When he saw Mia, he stopped and looked from her to Slade to Caleb, then back to his sister.

"I didn't expect to see you." He didn't wait for her to answer. "Let's put Caleb on the table here so I can get a good look at that nose."

Slade set his son on the paper-covered examining table. Jesse leaned Caleb's head back, looked close, sighed. "Caleb, this is going to hurt just a little, but I promise if you hang tight, it won't last long and Mia makes a pretty mean hot dog if you ask her real nice."

Mia mumbled something, but Caleb laughed so she smiled and let it go. Slade watched as Jesse touched and maneuvered his son's nose.

"It's cracked." Jesse finished his examination. "It

isn't too bad. We'll fix him up in just a few minutes and Mia can make him that hot dog."

"You're very funny." Mia spoke in quick Spanish to her brother and Jesse laughed.

"Hey, that's Spanish." Caleb's voice sounded a little nasal now.

"Yes, it is." Mia glared at Jesse. He said something again to her in Spanish.

Slade called a time-out. "Do you two think you could refrain from arguing in Spanish? It kind of makes a guy think you're talking about him."

Mia mouthed, "Sorry," and then she smiled at Caleb. "I can teach you Spanish if you'd like."

Caleb nodded. "Can I say something about a broken nose in Spanish? The kids would think that's cool."

"I think we can manage that."

"Do you really make good hot dogs?" His eyes narrowed. "'Cause I thought hot dogs were all the same."

"Jesse was teasing me because he knows I'm not a good cook."

"You made good cupcakes," Caleb offered.

"Thanks, Caleb."

A nurse brought in a clipboard with paperwork for Slade while Jesse taped Caleb's nose. Slade glanced at his son, who had reached for Mia's hand, holding tight.

"There you go, Caleb." Jesse held up a mirror. "Two black eyes, a cracked nose and a pretty skinned-up chin. Do you think maybe you shouldn't jump through a hoop again?"

Caleb grinned. "Next time I do, I won't fall."

Jesse laughed and Slade shook his head. "That's my son."

"Now can we have hot dogs?" Caleb took Jesse's hand as he hopped down from the table.

"Sorry about that," Jesse apologized and looked at his watch. "Got to go. You all have a good dinner. And Mia, I'll be by in a day or two."

"Sounds good." Mia held out her hand to Caleb. "Let's go have hot dogs at Vera's. Your dad's buying. And then you can have that cupcake for dessert."

"Shouldn't I get the cupcake now?" Caleb asked as they walked out of the room, leaving Slade with Jesse. "Because I broke my nose."

"I think you have a point. Let's go get that cupcake."

Slade shook his head and handed the clipboard back to Jesse.

"Good luck with her." Jesse pocketed his pen. "If you need anything at all, give me a call."

"Thanks. Do you have any advice on how to handle your grandmother?"

Jesse laughed an easy laugh and pointed to the ring on his finger. "If I had advice, it would be to trust her. I'm happier than I've ever been in my life. Has she offered you a ring?"

"She asked me to come by her house. She has something she wants me to haul off."

"Yes, that sounds like my grandmother trying to give away another heirloom ring. Don't worry, she doesn't take this job lightly. She puts a lot of prayer into her matchmaking."

Slade stood in the opening that led from the room. From there he could see the parking lot and he watched as Mia pulled a cupcake out of a box and gave it to his son. She laughed as Caleb licked frosting off the cupcake. Caleb offered her a bite and she shook her head.

"Maybe I'm partial because she's my sister, but she's a good person, Slade. She's tough. She's independent. Not every man can handle a woman like Mia."

"I'm not sure if I can." Slade tried not to smile—even he knew he failed. "I know you have to go. Thanks for taking care of Caleb."

"That's what I'm here for." Jesse excused himself and left.

Slade walked to the door that led out to the parking lot. For a minute he stayed inside, just watching as his son and Mia sat on the curb. Caleb licked the last of the cupcake off his fingers and then he saw Slade and waved.

He joined them in the parking lot. Mia held out the box, offering him the last cupcake. She smiled and he couldn't think past that smile that lit up her face. He couldn't get past how she'd held his son back at the school.

Somehow he and Caleb had gone from a duo to a trio that included Mia. And it felt right. At the same time it caused a big ache in his heart. Letting her in meant letting go.

Chapter Fifteen

Over the next week things settled into a routine that was easy to handle. Mia spent time with Tina. At home she searched for Breezy. She thought a lot about Slade, but she spent more time avoiding him. On a pretty Monday in October, Mia's mom took her to Tulsa for a doctor's appointment and then to the office to talk to her supervisor.

They discussed how Tina was doing and if there was anything more that could be done to protect her or to make her feel safe. Mia hadn't quite known what to say. She had replayed the day Butch got killed in her mind hundreds of times. She'd thought about what Nolan said about the money that had disappeared.

Mia's boss wanted to know if it was possible that Tina had the money. Mia doubted it. She didn't see Tina as a person who would put her kids in danger by keeping the money. And if she did have it, she wouldn't be hiding in Dawson in a single-wide trailer.

Someone had the money and Nolan Jacobs wanted it back. But he was smart enough not to come on his own. He would have other people do his dirty work.

The other thing Mia's boss had asked her was if

she planned to return to work. She had been placed on medical leave, but he wanted her back, if at all possible. Even if it meant reassigning her, or possibly transferring her to another division.

In another state.

Once she got back home, and after her mom left, Mia put on shorts and her running shoes. She walked outside. October had brought cooler weather, even some rain and she could feel fall in the air.

Mia stretched and then she started down the road, lengthening her stride, fighting past the ache in her arm. She breathed in the cool air, the scent of the country fields. She thought about leaving. She thought about staying. In each scenario that played through her mind she thought about Slade and Caleb.

She thought about not being enough for them. She'd been in their world. She'd walked through the halls of the school and she'd tried to play the part. As much as she'd loved playing the part, she didn't know if she fit the role.

It ached deep inside her, the idea of not fitting in. She knew how to play so many people, so why not play the part of someone who could fit into Slade and Caleb's life? Why couldn't that be who she really was, and not a role?

She thought about Tina because it was easier than dwelling on her own life. Tina had had more contractions today, but her new doctor said it could be another week. Since she arrived, there had been no signs that she'd been followed, that anyone knew where she was.

Mia pushed all the thoughts from her mind and focused on the sun setting on the horizon, sinking into the clouds and casting the sky in hazy, yellow light. A car came from behind her. It slowed and stopped.

Mia turned slowly, cautious until she saw the patrol car.

"Slade."

She hadn't spent a lot of time with him since the day at the emergency room. She didn't know if he'd been avoiding her or if he'd simply been busy. Maybe she'd avoided him.

"How did the appointment go?"

She stared out at the horizon where the sun was sinking. "Okay, I guess. The doctor isn't saying a lot. He thinks I'm healing better than he'd hoped for, but he doesn't think I'll get full use of my arm. My boss is pushing me to decide what I want to do."

"Do?"

"Where I want to work?" She looked back at him. "If I want to come back."

"That's a lot to think about."

"Yes, it is. I didn't think it would be this hard."

"To go back?"

She nodded and then she managed a smile to brighten the mood. "So what brought you out here?"

"I had something for you but you weren't home."

"No, I needed to get out and think."

"This isn't a good idea."

"Really?" She leaned to touch her toes and to draw in a deep breath. He took off his hat and tossed it on the seat of the patrol car. "Mia, please get in and let me drive you home."

"No, I can't. I'm going to finish my run."

"Then I'm going to follow you."

"I really wish you wouldn't. I don't need to be protected. You can go to the house and wait for me."

"I'm going to follow you." His jaw tensed. His brown

eyes caught and held hers. She wanted to give in to him, but she couldn't.

This felt like the line in the sand. She couldn't be the type of person he wanted her to be or needed her to be. "I'm jogging."

"Mia, get in the car."

She shook her head. She really wanted to get in that car with him, but stubborn pride and self-preservation joined efforts to keep her safe from the heartbreak sitting behind the wheel of that patrol car.

"What's wrong with you?" He stayed next to her as she kept going.

"I can't do this." She glanced his way, but kept running.

"Do what? Get in the car?"

She stood outside his car, looking down at him and wanting like mad to put her arms around him and hold on.

"I'm not a mom or a wife a man comes home to every night. I don't know how to be…"

She couldn't say *Vicki,* but he seemed to get it.

"Who asked you to be Vicki? Not me. I've never asked you to be anyone but yourself."

"Here you are, though, following me home."

"Because I don't want you to get hurt."

She leaned into the car and touched his cheek. He stared up at her and she kissed him softly and quickly.

"I'm not Vicki. I realized the other day at the school that I don't fit. I don't know how to talk to those women. I know how to outrun and outfight some of the toughest people in our society, but I can't talk about slow-cooker recipes."

"I didn't ask you to be anyone other than who you are."

"No, you didn't. This is about me and who I think I need to be. I can't fill her shoes."

"Let me give you a ride home. Please."

His calm voice took her by surprise. She'd expected anger or an argument, something other than this calm, rational person watching her.

She walked around and got in the car. Her heart raced, not because of the run. She held her right arm and breathed through the pain that shot up her shoulder, but it was nothing compared to the pain ripping into her heart.

"Mia, find out who you are. I think you'll like the person inside you. I know I do."

Doubt. She closed her eyes. When she opened them Slade was pulling into the driveway.

"I brought you something." His voice was still calm.

She looked at him and then at her house. She started to ask him what he'd brought and then she saw. The woman standing on her front porch wore a peasant skirt and a long flowing top. She had brown hair and glasses. A guitar case leaned against the side of the house.

"Breezy?"

"Yes. I found her for you. I checked out her story and then I bought her a plane ticket. I picked her up in Tulsa this afternoon."

"Slade." It hurt to say his name because she wanted to be the person he could love.

"Go, Mia. Don't say anything else. I think you've thrown enough at me for one night. I'm not sure who you think I am, but I do know who you are and I know what I want. Maybe someday you'll realize that what I want is you, and only you. I don't want you to be someone else. I'm not trying to replace Vicki."

"I don't know if I can be who you need me to be."

He reached across her and opened the car door. "Your sister is waiting."

Mia leaned and kissed his cheek. He sighed and shook his head.

"Thank you, Slade."

He nodded, but he didn't answer. Mia got out and as she walked up the sidewalk to face her sister for the first time in twenty years, Slade's car backed out of the drive.

"Mia?" Breezy stepped forward, her smile growing.

"Breezy. I've been looking for you."

"Slade told me."

"I want to know everything." Mia held her sister's hand. "We have a lot of time to make up for."

"I know." Breezy looked around. "And it looks like we've lived pretty different lives."

"Has your life been…"

Breezy smiled an easy smile. "My life has been fine. Maybe not like this, and I don't have a cowboy cop in love with me, but my life has been good."

They hugged and tears trickled down Mia's cheeks. She brushed them away, but more fell. She had her sister back. She shouldn't cry over that because it was the best gift anyone had ever given her. As they walked into the house she glanced toward the intersection at the end of her street and watched the patrol car pull onto the main road. She finally had her sister but she worried that maybe she'd just lost the one man she'd ever loved.

Slade sat down in a corner booth at Vera's. He picked up the menu, leaned back and ran a shaky hand through his hair. Man, what a day. He opened the menu more for something to do than to pick something. He knew what he wanted.

Mia.

No, this was about supper right now, not the woman who knew how to turn his life inside out and upside down. Chaos. That's what she was.

"Hey, cowboy, what are you doing eating alone?" Vera, the owner of the Mad Cow, sat down across from him and pulled out the order pad she carried in her apron. "My goodness, you look worse than a hundred dollars of old money."

"Thanks, Vera, I feel about that good."

"Saw you drive by earlier with a pretty girl. I didn't recognize her."

"It was a surprise for Mia."

"Well…" Vera looked shocked and then pulled it together. "Now I guess it would surprise Mia if she saw you running around with that young woman."

"It was Mia's sister."

"I've seen her sisters, and that young lady wasn't one of them."

"Her biological sister."

"Goodness, that is a surprise. Slade, you're one of a kind. Now what can I get you for supper, because I'm all out of smiles and you seem to be missing yours, considering you just gave a girl the gift of a lifetime."

"Yeah, well, that's how things go sometimes, Vera."

"How about if your fried chicken is on the house tonight?"

He smiled at that. "Vera, you don't have to."

"I know, but I want to. You know, I like to take care of the local law. They take good care of me."

The cowbells over the door chimed. Slade didn't turn around, because it was Dawson and he'd know whoever it was walking into the diner. A few seconds later Jackson sat down across from him.

"Boy, you look like one hundred dollars…"

Slade raised a hand to stop him. "Don't. Vera already told me. Nothing a good night's rest won't cure."

"Let me buy your dinner." Jackson picked up the menu. "Mia has already been on the phone with Mom. Seems we have a new Cooper and you're responsible."

"Don't you have a wife and kids to eat dinner with?"

"They're in Tulsa for the ballet. It's a mother-daughter thing while Aunt Heather keeps the baby. I can guarantee you I'm glad it isn't a father-daughter thing because I can do without ballet."

"Gotcha."

"Lucky for you I have nothing but time."

"Lucky me."

Jackson looked over the menu and when Vera wandered over he ordered a chef's salad. Vera wrote it down, gave the two of them a curious look and left.

"How'd you find her?"

"A little digging, some police records and, bingo, Breezy. Don't worry, a very small police record and nothing to send up any alarms over."

"Where's she been?"

"California. She and her grandmother were street musicians. Her grandmother died a couple of years ago. Since then Breezy has been on her own. She has no real education, but she's smart. I think she's been homeless part of the time."

"Rough life."

"You would think so, but she seems pretty happy."

"That's good. That makes you Mia's hero."

"I don't think that's exactly the case."

Vera brought their food and for a second seemed like she might say something. She shook her head and refrained. Slade smiled as she walked away.

"Vera's having a hard time not giving advice." He reached for the pepper shaker.

"She probably wants to tell you that your cholesterol is going to be through the roof if you don't have a salad once in a while."

"My cholesterol levels are fine and I do eat salad. Thanks for the public service announcement."

"I do have a brother who is a doctor."

"Right. That makes you almost a professional."

Jackson dug into his salad and Slade was glad to have his friend otherwise occupied for at least five minutes. When they finished eating, Slade would make a good excuse and escape.

Unfortunately, Jackson was as stubborn as his sister and everyone else in the Cooper family. Slade figured it had to be a learned trait, because they all had it, adopted and biological. That many kids in a family would cause a person to stand his ground.

"Slade, I don't know what's going on with you and my sister."

"Well, Jackson, that makes two of us. And I don't really need a lecture about keeping my distance and not hurting her. You threatened me about fifteen years ago, if I remember correctly. I took it to heart then because our friendship meant a lot to me. Right now, I don't care to hear it."

Jackson held both hands up in surrender and laughed a little. "Whoa, don't go all John Wayne on me. I was just going to say, I wish you luck. She's as mule-headed as they come and when she gets something in her mind, it's hard for her to let go."

"You don't say."

"If you need to talk or want advice…"

"No, I don't think I do." Slade pushed aside his plate

and finished off his tea. "My mom has been in Grove with Caleb. I need to get home and check on them."

"Right. And don't worry, it'll all work out."

"Thanks, Dear Abby."

Jackson picked up his tab and followed Slade to the register. "No problem, Lovelorn. I hope it works out for you."

"Nice, real nice."

Vera hurried to the register, wiping her hands on her apron as she walked. "Slade, I already told you, this is on me. Jackson, you need to learn to chew your food."

"Thanks, Vera." Slade waved and walked out the door, the cowbells clanking behind him.

He considered driving back up the street past Mia's, but thought about how that would look, him cruising past like some lovesick teen. No, he'd head on home to Caleb because he didn't need to live up to Jackson's nickname of *Lovelorn*.

Before he headed home, he turned on the little street that led to Myrna Cooper's house. He knew what she wanted to give him and he guessed he might as well tell her that this wasn't the right time.

Chapter Sixteen

Mia woke up Tuesday morning to the smell of bacon frying. She rolled over and moved her arm, letting it rest on the pillow next to her. The radio was playing in the kitchen and someone was singing along. Mia rolled over quickly and fumbled in the drawer of the bedside table for her weapon.

And then she remembered. Breezy.

She hurried down the hall and into the kitchen. Her sister stood in front of the stove, something wonderful and cheesy in the pan. She turned and smiled a big smile.

"Good morning. You slept late. I've been up since dawn, thinking that this is the most beautiful place on earth. There wasn't a sound, just birds and cows and that horse of yours."

Mia hugged her sister and snatched a piece of bacon from the plate next to the stove. Breezy used the spatula to move more bacon to the plate.

"I guess it is quiet after living in Los Angeles." Mia poured herself a glass of milk. "You cook. That makes you the perfect roommate."

"You have a house. That makes you even better."

Breezy said it with a smile but Mia had to wonder if it had been that easy, wandering, living off what they earned singing on street corners and sometimes being homeless.

"I'm so glad you're here."

"Me, too." Breezy flipped the omelet onto a plate and cut it in half. "I hope you don't mind my taking over. I was starving."

"No, please, take over."

"Can we sit outside? I know it's a little cool but I love that view."

"Of grass and trees?"

"Yes. And your horse. Can you ride her?"

"Yes. I put a saddle on her the other day and rode her for a few minutes. She's a sweetheart."

The doorbell chimed. Breezy grabbed their plates and headed for the door. "You get it. I'll be waiting for you."

Mia hurried through the house, peeking out the living room window before opening the door. She ignored the letdown when it wasn't Slade's truck parked in her driveway. But, of course, it wouldn't be Slade. Not after yesterday.

It was better this way.

Her mom stood on the front porch, looking pretty and fresh in jeans and a long-sleeved shirt. Young. Angie Cooper always seemed young. Mia hugged her mom and invited her in.

"I want to meet Breezy. I'm sorry, I should have waited but I couldn't."

"You don't have to wait." Mia motioned her inside. "Do you want coffee? Breezy made a pot."

"No, I've had plenty. Is that breakfast I smell?"

"Don't look so hopeful, I'm not cooking. Breezy cooks."

"Wonderful."

They walked out the back door and Breezy looked up, smiling a bright, open smile. She stood and hugged Angie Cooper.

"Breezy, I'm so glad you're here." Angie pointed to their plates. "Sit and eat. I don't want your breakfast to get cold."

"Thank you." Breezy sat back down.

Angie took the seat next to Mia, touching her arm and smiling. "This is so exciting. Slade did this?"

"Yes, he did." Mia looked down at her plate.

"He knew that Mia was looking for me." Breezy filled in, giving Mia a frown and then carrying on for her. "He bought my plane ticket and yesterday afternoon picked me up in Tulsa."

"Well, isn't he amazing." Angie continued to study Mia.

"Yes, amazing." Mia took another bite of omelet.

"Well, Mia, you have a lot to think about." Angie didn't beat around the bush. "Your sister is here. You have opportunities at work."

Mia waited, holding her breath, praying her mom wouldn't put Slade on the list of things she had to think about. And she didn't.

"Yes, a lot to think about," Mia agreed. She looked at her watch. "I just remembered, Tina has a doctor's appointment today. If she doesn't have the baby in the next week they're going to induce labor."

"Do you need me to take her to Grove?" Angie offered.

"No, I should do it. Jackson brought me their little

car. It's an automatic. No shifting." She smiled at her little sister. "You can come with me."

"No, I'll stay here, if you don't mind. I thought I'd clean house and put something on for dinner."

"Cook? Twice in one day?" Mia loved the idea. "Sounds wonderful. There's a freezer in the garage. There should be plenty of meat. I usually end up taking half of it to the food pantry because I can't use everything Jackson shoves in there."

"I'll make good use of it." Breezy picked up their plates. "I'm going to wash the dishes."

"Breezy, you don't have to do that. You can rest."

Breezy stopped at the door. "No, Mia, I want to do this. It's been a long time since I've had a home, a kitchen like this. This is a joy, not a chore."

"Okay, but don't feel as if you have to. And if you decide you don't want to cook, there's always the Mad Cow."

"I don't know how that could be good."

Mia laughed. "It's the local café."

"Oh!" And then Breezy was gone and Mia tried not to look at her mom.

"You okay?" Angie turned her chair to face Mia. "For someone who has her sister and possibly her job back, you don't seem happy."

"I messed up."

"How?"

Mia closed her eyes and shook her head. "I thought for a little while that I could be someone I'm not."

"Someone you're not?" Angie cleared her throat. "I happen to think you can be anything you want."

"I know you do." Mia smiled at the often-used encouragement. "But I'm not the person who…"

She couldn't even say it. Angie waited. Patient. With

twelve kids, she'd had more than her share of these conversations.

"I'm not mom material. I can't cook. I have a dangerous job. I take chances."

"Are you planning on having kids?"

Mia looked up. "No, I'm not. I just can't fill the shoes of someone who…"

"In your opinion, the shoes of someone who walked on water?"

Ouch. "Vicki knew how to be a mom. She had the wife thing down. It was all she ever wanted."

"So you're going to run from what you want because you don't think you can fill someone else's shoes? Mia, you have your own shoes. You do just fine in them."

"Right, but my shoes tend to take me places that aren't always pretty."

"Maybe it's time for you to try on new shoes."

Mia smiled at that. Her phone rang, interrupting the conversation. "It's Tina. She probably thinks I've forgotten."

"Mia, there's someone outside," Tina said. "Slade isn't home. His mom went somewhere. I think to visit his sister."

"Do you recognize the car? It could be someone looking for Slade."

"No, I don't think so."

"Okay, keep the doors locked. I'll be there in five minutes."

"I'm calling 911." And the phone went dead.

"I have to go." Mia explained the conversation as she ran to the door.

"Mia, call Slade."

"I'll call him on my way." She hurried to her room, quickly slipping her feet into shoes she felt comfortable with and loading the weapon she kept in her bed-side table.

"Mia, why don't you wait?" Her mom followed her out the garage door.

"Because I can't leave her out there alone, and Mom, these are the shoes I know how to wear. This is my job."

"Right. I'll pray."

Mia hit the button to raise the garage door. "I know you will. Those prayers get me through a lot of hard times."

A few minutes later she was on the road, but she knew she couldn't go in the front way to Slade's. She would take a back road and go through the field to get to the trailer. With any luck a county deputy would go up the drive and distract whoever was at the house.

Mia parked the car on the shoulder of the road. She left the keys but holstered her weapon. She had about ten acres to cover. She slid through the barbed wire of the fence and surveyed the land. The best way was along the fence row. There were even a few trees that would somewhat hide her from view.

As she got closer to the house she could see the Jeep parked in front of the trailer and two men. How had they found Tina's location? Mia pulled her gun from the holster at her waist and eased along the fence. She knew the lay of the land, the outbuildings, even pos-sible escape routes. She had the upper hand. But they had her outnumbered.

As she eased behind an equipment shed someone yelled. She heard a shot. They were at the back of the trailer, shooting the door handle. Mia stepped out from behind the shed and raised her gun to fire but one of them spotted her, and was distracted from going inside.

He raised his weapon to fire. Before she could react,

a body slammed her from the side, sending her to the hard-packed ground. The shot fired over their heads.

"Slade." She rolled over and he rolled next to her. They were both breathing hard, trying to get their air back. "How?"

"No time." He stood, and raised his weapon. "Stop."

The man on the porch raised a gun, leveled it at Slade. Mia pulled her weapon but she couldn't do it. Her fingers couldn't make the connections they needed to make.

Slade fired. The man on the back porch fell.

The other man came down off the steps, his hand on his weapon. Slade kept his weapon aimed. "Don't do it."

Sirens sounded in the distance and Mia could see the flashing lights. She could see the guy considering his options and then he dropped his weapon.

Mia dropped her gun at her side and watched as Slade hurried forward to cuff the men. He called for an ambulance and then he hurried up the steps and inside the house.

Mia moved more slowly, picking up her weapon and holstering it. She walked up the back steps of the house. The wounded man held his leg. A paramedic had already rounded the corner of the trailer.

Inside the trailer she found Tina on the sofa, her knees drawn up, her face pale. The kids were next to her, one on each side.

"Tina." Mia knelt in front of her.

"My water just broke." Tina started to shake. "I'm going to have a baby. There are men trying to kill me and I don't know why."

Mia reached for the kids. "Tina, we need to stay calm. Let's talk about the baby and about what you're going to name him. Let's think about tomorrow and how much better life is going to be."

She turned and looked at Slade. He didn't smile. He didn't say anything. Not to her.

"Tina, we have a second ambulance here. They're going to take you to the hospital." Slade had holstered his gun and he was smiling at Tina in a reassuring way that made even Mia feel better.

"My kids?" Tina stopped talking and her face scrunched with pain.

Slade sat down next to her. "Breathe. You have to breathe. The kids are fine. Mia and I will take them to the hospital."

"Mia has to go in with me. I can't do this alone."

Mia's eyes widened. Go into the delivery room? See a baby born? She didn't know if she could. But then she looked at Tina. If Tina could have this baby without Butch, Mia could hold her hand through labor and delivery.

"We'll be there, Tina." Mia squeezed her arm gently. "It will only take us a few minutes to get there. We'll be right behind you."

Tina nodded and the paramedic helped her to her feet. He walked her out the door, stopping before they went down the steps. Mia watched as Tina grasped the man's hand and held tight. After a long minute they continued.

"I need to talk to the sheriff," Slade said as he walked to the door. "Can you get the kids some snacks and maybe toys? We'll use my car to get to the hospital. My patrol car is in the neighbor's field."

That's how he had gotten to her side so quickly. Because they'd had the same idea about approaching from behind the house.

Mia nodded and, with Tina's frightened kids at her side, she filled a backpack with toys and then shoved snacks in on top.

"Can we have some of those?"

Jackie pointed to a jar with cookies inside. Jars posed a problem. Mia nodded but when she tried to work the lid, her hand didn't have the strength. Slade walked through the front door, saw what she was doing and took the jar from her.

He opened it and held it down for the kids to each get a cookie.

"Ready to go?"

Mia nodded. The kids were still holding tight to her. She slipped the backpack over her shoulder and they each took a hand.

"The sheriff wants to know why you were here." Slade spoke as they walked down the steps.

"Tina called me. I didn't know how long it would take someone to get here, so I decided to come in from the back."

"Good thinking that almost got you killed."

"But it didn't."

"No, it didn't."

Because he'd had the same idea and he'd been there to save her. An answer to her mother's prayers? Mia sighed and opened the back door of the sedan to let the kids climb in.

"Seat belts." Because they didn't have booster seats. Jackie pulled the belt over her brother and then buckled herself in.

Slade watched as Mia got in and reached for her own seat belt. Without asking, he reached over and took it from her, easily clicking it into place. Mia closed her eyes against the pounding frustration, the loss, the ebbing denial because she could no longer deny.

When they walked through the doors of the hospital, Jesse greeted them. "Mia, this way. She's ready to have this baby now."

"Now? Shouldn't it take longer?" Mia followed him down the hall to the wing labeled Labor and Delivery. "Don't I need to scrub or gown up, or something?"

"Wash your hands." He pointed to a sink.

As she washed, he grabbed surgical scrubs off a shelf. "Here you go, sis. And try to smile. Birth is a beautiful thing."

"I'm sure it's beautiful." She thought there would be other words to describe it, but she let him go with *beautiful* because it made him smile like a crazy, in love loon.

He and his wife, Laura, were already planning to have a big family. He pulled Mia from her thoughts, telling her she had to hurry—Tina was asking for her.

Mia walked through the wide door of the room that Jesse indicated. "Going."

Tina reached for Mia's hand as soon as she saw her. Mia let her squeeze. She helped her breathe. She didn't know the steps, but the nurse on the other side of the bed guided them both through the process, smiling encouragingly and telling them what to do next.

Mia thought about finding an escape. Obviously, the very calm and comforting nurse could help Tina more than she could. But Tina held on tight and somehow Mia forgot that she wanted to leave, that she didn't want to be in the middle of the birth of Tina's baby.

When the baby came into the world, a crying mess, purple-red and fisting the air, Mia fell in love. She fell in love with the way that little boy's eyes scrunched and then opened. She fell in love with the way Tina held him close and called him Alexander, Butch's real name. She fell in love even deeper when the nurse wrapped him in a blanket and Tina closed her eyes and asked Mia to hold him.

She held that baby boy close and he made mewling sounds and cried pitifully for his mommy.

Tina opened her eyes, smiled and then cried. "Mia, I have a baby. What do I do with him, with my life?"

Mia placed the baby next to Tina. "You love him. You teach him about his dad. You stay in Dawson where you have people who will help you. And you find healing."

"I haven't felt so alone since the day they told me."

"I know." Mia sat next to Tina and held her hand tight. "I'm so sorry, Tina. I tried."

"You have to forgive yourself. You didn't do this. You couldn't change it."

"I wanted to." Mia placed a hand on the baby. "But I'm here and we'll get through this."

Tina nodded, but her eyes were drooping. "Thank you."

Mia walked out the door while the pediatrician examined Alexander and the doctor finished with Tina. She saw Slade in the waiting room with Jackie and Jason. He looked up and smiled a soft smile. She wanted to go to him, to curl into his hug and feel whole again.

But instead she walked down the hall away from him.

Slade left the kids with Angie Cooper, who had showed up at the hospital to check on Tina and Mia. It was Mia he particularly wanted to talk to at the moment. He hurried down the hall and out the side door that led to a courtyard.

She stood next to a fountain, the breeze blowing her hair. She held her right arm. The gun that had been in the holster was now locked in his car.

When he walked up beside her, she turned and smiled.

"It's a boy. She named him Alexander. He's beautiful."

"You did good today. Other than that part where you put yourself in a lot of danger."

"I had to protect her. I promised Butch."

"But I have to protect you. I don't want you hurt."

She exhaled slowly and stared again at the fountain. "Slade, I've been taking care of myself for a long time."

"Does that mean you can't let anyone else take care of you?"

"I don't know what it means. I do know that someone I trusted must have leaked information about Tina's location."

"That's true. They arrested a guy in the Tulsa DEA office. It seems he might have had a guy inside Nolan Jacobs's operation. The guy told him that Butch had met with Tina. When they got the chance, they stole Nolan's money and blamed it on Butch. That's why Nolan had his thugs come after the two of you. He was convinced one of you had his money."

"That's why Nolan wanted his money that day? Butch and I didn't know what he was talking about. But he also knew that we were cops."

"Yeah."

"It makes sense, but I wish it didn't."

"Mia, I miss you."

She smiled at him then. "I miss you, too. But Slade, who do you want me to be?"

"What does that mean?"

"I'm not sure who you want me to be. This is who I am. I've been on my own a long time. I can make a great salad. I have running shoes, not high heels. I stood in Caleb's classroom and I felt like a fraud. I was the undercover agent posing as a class mom."

"How did it feel, when you played that part?"

"It was a part, Slade."

"How did it feel, Mia?"

She shook her head, refusing to answer.

He wanted to shake her to make her see sense. But he knew Mia. She had to wrap her mind around something. No one was going to push her to the right answer. As much as he wanted to pull her into his arms and convince her that what they had was real, and who she was in that classroom was real, he knew he couldn't.

"Are you leaving?" He had to ask.

As much as he didn't want to hear the answer, he had to know.

She stared at the fountain for a long time and finally she shrugged. "I don't know. They offered me a new assignment."

"New assignment where, Mia?"

"East Coast."

"We'll miss you."

She looked up again, brushing her hair back from her face with her left hand. "I didn't say I was going."

"I'm going to be praying you make the right choice. And that you realize who you are to me."

"Who am I to you?"

"The person I love." He touched her cheek. "Who am I to you?"

She smiled. "The person I love. The person I've always loved."

"Then why does this have to be so hard, Mia?"

"Because a little piece of me would always feel like I was stepping into Vicki's shoes."

"She wasn't perfect." He eased the words out, not wanting to sound as if he wasn't loyal to the woman he had loved. "She couldn't make gravy. She always made coffee too strong. And she didn't like my job. But I loved her. She loved me. Neither of us was perfect."

"I need time."

"I'll give you time." He brushed his hand through her hair, feeling soft, silky strands wrap around his fingers. He inhaled her scent and then he leaned to kiss her. "I'll give you time because both of us need time to deal with this."

As he walked away, he wondered how it had happened that the woman who had been a pretty kid he'd spent his childhood with had become the woman he wanted to spend the rest of his life with.

He looked back before walking through the door. She had turned to watch him and she smiled.

He nodded and walked in as Jesse walked out, giving them both a look but not asking questions. Slade didn't need more questions than the ones he was already asking himself.

Chapter Seventeen

Two weeks after Tina's son was born, Slade watched as Mia left her house to go jogging. He waited until she was safely out of sight before he knocked on the door. Breezy let him in. She shook her head at the big box he carried in with him.

"You really think this is romantic?" She watched as he opened the box and took out the contents.

"I think it's necessary."

"You could sit on the front porch and tell her you heard she's no longer an agent and maybe she'd like to, I don't know, hang out some time?"

"That doesn't sound much better than my plan."

"Well, do what you have to do, cowboy. I'm just saying, this is corny. I'd try flowers and maybe a candle-light dinner."

"Does that sound like your sister?"

She laughed and slipped her feet into sandals. "Nope. I'm going down to Vera's. She's offered me a job. Oh, and she's going to have live music on Saturdays. It feels a little like charity, but since I love to sing, I'll take the gig."

"Breezy, thanks for helping out."

"No problem, but don't blame me if she shoots you. She's getting pretty good at being a lefty."

"Thanks for the warning."

He watched as she headed down the sidewalk in the direction of Vera's. He liked Breezy. He still wasn't sure about her, but he liked her. He wrote it off to being a cop and always being a little suspicious.

Mia would be back soon. He knew that what he was about to do was bordering on corny, but a guy did what a guy had to do. And his son had informed him yesterday that he missed Mia and wished his dad would get her back before the next party at school.

Slade had promised to do his best.

He arranged everything on the coffee table, building something of a pyramid. When he saw her coming up the sidewalk, he touched his pocket and felt the ring. Myrna had insisted he take it. The ruby ring was what she'd wanted hauled out of her house. He'd expected an old appliance.

Casual. He wanted to be casual when she walked through the door. It was hard to be casual with sweaty palms and a rapidly beating heart.

The door opened. She paused when she saw him but then she walked in, staring first at him and then at his display. She shook her head and even smiled. After a few seconds she laughed.

"What are you doing here, Slade?"

Mia looked at the man standing in front of her, wearing his best jeans, a button-up shirt, with his cowboy hat in his hands. He looked as nervous as a kid on his first date. Not that she'd had many first dates. She hadn't dated much at all.

She'd been waiting. Her heart skipped a beat and

then raced to catch up. She'd been waiting for what she thought she could never have. And then she'd felt guilty for wanting what belonged to someone else.

She'd been waiting. She'd made a promise to God as a teen and she'd kept the promise.

"Mia."

"Slade.

"I came here today to bring you some shoes."

She had noticed. She smiled at him and then at the pyramid of shoe boxes. "That's a strange gift to bring a woman."

"I would have brought roses, but shoes seem to be the problem."

"I don't know what to do, Slade."

"I do, Mia. I know what to do. I know that I thought my heart wouldn't have room to love anyone else. And then you came back with your mule-headed independence."

"That's romantic." She wiped at her eyes.

"You came back." He stepped close, pulling her to him. "And you opened my heart up again. I realized that hearts don't run out of room to love. God gives us new dreams, new plans. He sees our emptiness and knows exactly what it's going to take to fill us up again."

"I'm going to cry." She touched his cheek and kissed him, sweetly savoring his taste.

Slade moved back just a step and smiled. "I brought you shoes. Every single pair is your size. Running shoes, boots, sandals, you name it, you can wear them all. There are some mom shoes, some wife-looking shoes. Some shoes that I think would be pretty sexy on your long legs."

She started to laugh and he laughed, too.

"That's about the corniest thing I've ever heard, Slade McKennon."

"You were worried about filling shoes that weren't yours. I wanted you to know that you aren't playing a part, Mia. You're everything. You are tough when you need to be tough, but you held my son and fixed him cupcakes when he needed that. And you knew what he needed when I didn't. You are a woman worthy of many pairs of shoes."

She laughed and sniffled. He offered her a tissue.

"I can do better than corny." He reached into his pocket. "I can do romantic."

"Can you?" She held her breath when he held out the ruby-and-diamond ring.

"I can."

He kneeled in front of her and reached for her hand. He slipped the ring on her finger and it fit perfectly. "I want you to marry me. I want you to be Caleb's mom and my wife, and I want to have more kids. With you. Because I love you."

"Slade."

He stopped her. "Mia, Caleb sent me on a mission today. He said I need to fix things before his next school party. So before you argue, I want you to realize that Caleb loves you, too."

"I love you both."

She curled her fingers around his and pulled him to his feet and then she walked into his arms. His lips claimed hers, searching her heart, searching for the love they both knew they shared. It was a gift, this love, and Mia would never take it for granted.

Slade whispered her name and then he kissed her a second time, stealing her breath, crashing her defenses, scattering all her doubts. His hands held her close and she felt safe.

"Marry me?"

She nodded and whispered, "Which shoes should I wear?"

"I like the idea of you barefoot."

They laughed and kissed again.

Epilogue

The wedding march started to play. Mia stood next to her dad. Tim Cooper smiled, but his eyes watered with unshed tears as he lowered the veil to cover her face.

"This is it, honey. I pray for you a long life with Slade, with all of God's blessings. Love each other well, forgive often and make me a grandpa again." He kissed her cheek.

"Oh, Dad." She couldn't cry, she'd smear the makeup that Heather had so lovingly applied.

They watched as the bridesmaids, all of her sisters, and the groomsmen, led by Caleb, took their places at the front of the church. The bridesmaids were dressed in palest pink and carried white roses. The spring wedding seemed to call for simple elegance. Mia had surprised her sisters with that word.

Slade stood in the center of them, his smile reaching back to her as she started down the aisle on her father's arm.

A moment later Mia joined him at the front of the church. He wore a Western-cut suit that made the best of his broad shoulders. She wore her mother's wedding dress and Granny Myrna's veil.

And no shoes. Because it had been their joke and she'd stuck with it. She was the barefoot bride. But in her suitcase, packed away for the honeymoon, were the shoes that Slade thought would look sexy on her.

The most amazing thing was the man standing in front of her. His smile captivated her heart. His love sealed the deal. She closed her eyes and said a silent thank-you because God had known and brought them together.

Next to her, Breezy sighed. It meant everything to have her standing with Mia's other sisters. Caleb was the best man, in every way possible. He looked proud of his role and he'd informed them just a few days ago that he expected a little brother or sister pretty soon. He was going to be six soon and he didn't mince words.

Mia smiled at Caleb as Slade recited the vows. He was the child of her heart. He winked at her and she winked back.

Minister Wyatt Johnson spoke the final words of the ceremony, pronouncing them husband and wife, then told Slade to kiss his bride. Slade grinned and pulled her close. He wrapped his arms around her and kissed her cheek.

Mia growled a little warning. He kissed her other cheek.

She took matters into her own hands, pulling him close, holding him as she sealed their wedding with a kiss that made a few people gasp.

When she ended the kiss, Slade looked a little shocked. She leaned in close and whispered, "I've been waiting for you my whole life."

"Mia McKennon, I'm so glad you waited."

* * * * *

*If you enjoyed this story by Brenda Minton,
be sure to check out the other books
this month from Love Inspired!*

Dear Reader,

Each Cooper Creek story is a new adventure for me, and I hope for you, as well. Mia took me by surprise. She loves her family, but to put the pieces of her life and heart together, she needs to find her biological sister. This is a journey that many adopted children find themselves taking. It doesn't mean they love their adoptive family any less—it just means that they need to find the missing pieces of themselves.

It's the same journey that we take when we seek a relationship with God through Jesus. We sense that missing piece of ourselves that is found in that relationship, adopted into the family of God. It's a special gift that God gives us. It is a special gift we give a child.

Happy reading,

Brenda Minton

Questions for Discussion

1. We all handle grief differently. From the beginning we see that Mia is trying to figure out how to handle hers. Is she truly a person who has lost faith?

2. Why has this situation shaken her faith?

3. Slade is a widower with a young son. Does it make sense that he would be cautious in dating? How do you think he has handled his grief?

4. Is Mia running from her family or merely needing time alone to gather her thoughts without too many other voices telling her how to feel?

5. If Slade has kept his son and his dating life separate, why is Mia a safe zone for his child?

6. Slade's wife, Vicki, was Mia's best friend. Growing up, Slade was a friend of Vicki's. How does this affect their relationship going forward?

7. When is it apparent to Mia and Slade that there is more between them than friendship?

8. Why would Slade have kept pictures of Vicki from Caleb? Was it intentional, or one of those situations a parent never quite knows the right time or place for?

9. Does the attraction take them by surprise?

10. At times both Mia and Slade feel guilty for their feelings. Why?

11. Mia admits to Slade that she is waiting for marriage to give herself to the man she marries. How does he see her after this revelation?

12. Mia is worried about losing her job, but is the job really what she wants?

13. Did Mia take her job in law enforcement because she really wanted that career, or for other reasons?

14. Slade wants to protect Mia, but she makes it difficult. Is there a middle ground for two strong-willed people?

15. Slade knows he is in love with Mia, but he needs space. She needs space, too. Why?

16. Slade proposes with shoes—possibly the corniest proposal ever, but he wants to make a point. Not only does he love Mia, but how does he see her?

REQUEST YOUR FREE BOOKS!

2 FREE INSPIRATIONAL NOVELS
PLUS 2
FREE
MYSTERY GIFTS

Love Inspired®

Jolie followed Morgan outside. There was a large gnarled oak tree still bent over as it had been all those years ago. She didn't stop until she reached it, turning his way only after they were beneath the wide expanse of limbs.

Morgan crossed his arms and studied the tree. "I remember having to climb up this tree and talk you down after you scrambled up to the top and froze."

She hadn't expected him to bring up old memories—it caught her a little off guard. "I remember how mad you were at having to rescue the silly little new girl."

A hint of a smile teased his lips, fraying Jolie's nerves at the edges. It had been a long time since she'd seen that smile.

"I got used to it, though," he said, his voice warming.

Electricity hummed between them as they stared at each other. Jolie sucked in a wobbly breath. Then the hardness in Morgan's tone matched the accusation in his eyes.

"What are you doing here, Jolie? Why aren't you taming rapids in some far off place?"

"I…I'm—" She stumbled over her words. "I'm taking a leave from competition for a little while. I had a bad run in Virginia." She couldn't bring herself to say that she'd almost died. "Your dad offered me this teaching opportunity."

"I heard about the accident and I'm real sorry about that, Jolie," Morgan said. "But why come here after all this time?"

"This is my *home*."

Jolie saw anger in Morgan's eyes. Well, he had a right to it, and more than a right to point it straight at her.

But she'd thought she'd prepared for it.

She was wrong.

"Morgan," Jolie said, almost as a whisper. "I'd hoped we could forget the past and move forward."

Heart pounding, she reached across the space between them and placed her hand on his arm. It was just a touch, but the feeling of connecting with Morgan McDermott again after so much time rocked her straight to her core, and suddenly she wasn't so sure coming home had been the right thing to do after all.

Will Morgan ever allow Jolie back into his life—and his heart?

Pick up HER UNFORGETTABLE COWBOY
available May 2013 from Love Inspired Books.

Will You Marry Me?

Bold widow Johanna Yoder stuns Roland Byler when she asks him to be her husband. To Johanna, it seems very sensible that they marry. She has two children, he has a son. Why shouldn't their families become one? But the widower has never forgotten his long-ago love for her; it was his foolish mistake that split them apart. This could be a fresh start for both of them—until she reveals she wants a marriage of convenience only. It's up to Roland to woo the stubborn Johanna and convince her to accept him as her groom in her home and in her heart.

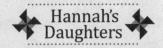

Johanna's Bridegroom

by

Emma Miller

Available May 2013

www.LoveInspiredBooks.com

LI8781